Areebah's Dilemma: Love or Deen

Karimah Grayson

First Edition June 2015
Second Edition July 2015
Third Edition August 2015
Fourth Edition September 2015

ISBN: 1514807025
ISBN-13: 978-1514807026

DEDICATION

To my husband, Tony L. Grayson, Sr., your support is greatly appreciated. For that, I dedicate this book to you.

Contents

ACKNOWLEDGMENTS

Indeed, all praises belong to Allah. I praise Him and seek His help and forgiveness. I seek refuge in Allah from my soul's evils and my wrong doings. He whom Allah guides, no one can misguide; and he whom He misguides, no one can guide. – Reported by Ibn Mas'ud and Ibn 'Abbas in Sahih Muslim.

I thank and acknowledge the following people and organizations for the inspiration and support in this work. My mother, Saeyda Quaye, I know she would have enjoyed this book. To my husband, Tony Grayson, Sr., I appreciate your support and kind words. To my sister, Sister Shelyta Van Horn of Tranquility Wearable Art, you always have my back. To my brother Augustus Van Horn, III, I appreciate all of your support and you always have my back. In remembrance to my brother Masai Cetewayo Lewis Joyner, gone but not forgotten. To my youngest brother Ayitey Quaye, keep on moving, Ummi would be proud of you. To my best friends, Doreen Merritt and Jennifer Wallace, thank you for the feedback and support. To all my children, Mika'eel, Tony, II, Kamilah, and Naimah, I love you all. To my grandchildren, Tahkeel and Camari, always strive for the best. To my students, old and new, thank you for allowing me to share my knowledge with you. To my coworkers at Sun Ed Margate thank you for the support. To Stephen McCrae, thank you for being the eBookman.

Islamic Terms & Meanings

Abi – my father

Alhamdulillah – all praises belong to Allah

Allah subhana wa ta'ala - The One God glorified and exalted

As salaamu alaikum – peace be upon you

Astaghfirullah Rabbi wa Atuubu Ilayh - Forgive me Allah, my Lord and accept my repentance.

Bismillahir Rahmanir Raheem - In the name of Allah the Most Gracious, the Most Merciful

Dhikr - remembrance

du'as – supplications

Halal – good; permitted

In shaa Allah – if it's the will of Allah

Inna illahi wa inna ilaihi raji'un - Verily from Allah we come and to Him we return

Janazah – funeral prayer

La hawla quwatta ilah billah – There is no power or might greater than Allah.

Maa shaa Allah - The will of Allah

PBUH – Peace Be Upon Him

Qur'an – holy scripture in Islam

Salatul 'Istikhara – a prayer made when making important decisions in one's life

SubhanAllah – Glory to Allah

Qadr Allah – the divine will of Allah

Surah – verse of the Qur'an

Ummi – my mother

Wa laikum mus salaam – and upon you be peace

Ya Allah - Oh Allah

One

Ring. Ring. Ring.

"As salaamu alaikum," Areebah said as she answered the phone.

"Hello," the voice on the other line said.

"Yes, hello," said Areebah becoming nervous as she looked at the caller ID and saw County Hospital.

"Is this Mrs. Wali?"

"Yes," she said still confused about the phone call, "Who is this?"

"I'm a nurse from the County Hospital."

"The County Hospital? May I ask what you are calling in reference to?" She said sitting straight up in the bed.

"Your husband has been admitted to the hospital. He wanted me to call you because he wants you to come be with him."

"The hospital! For what?"

"He's having some tests performed. Unfortunately due to patient confidentiality, I am unable to say anything else regarding his condition."

"Okay, I'll be there shortly. What is his room number? Is there anything I need to bring?" She shot questions at the nurse without taking a breath. She didn't know what to do. Fear crept into her thoughts and chills ran down her spine.

"His room number is 1122. When you arrive at the hospital, just go to the information desk and give them his name and room number they will give you a pass and let you know how to get to his room."

"Okay, thank you. Please take good care of my husband," she said as tears streamed down her face.

Sitting in the dark room, she sat up and began smoothing down her clothing. Just as she was about to leave, the adhan – call to prayer began. She decided to offer Salatul 'Asr – late afternoon prayer before leaving for the hospital. She prayed and made sincere du'a, that her husband would be fine. She's been concerned about him for some time. He's been losing weight and having angry outbursts for no reason. Therefore, in her heart, she felt that when she arrived at the hospital she would receive devastating news.

"As salaamu alaikum Sahlah, I'm going to the County Hospital. Your father has been admitted. I don't know anything else. I'll call you as soon as I receive more information," Areebah left this message on her daughter's voicemail as she drove to the hospital. She then called Baqir, their only son.

"As salaamu alaikum Baqir."

"Wa laikum mus salaam Ummi. How are you?"

"I'm praising Allah and saying Allahu Akbar (Allah is the Greatest). How are you?"

"I'm good, alhamdulillah (all praises belong to Allah), and to what pleasure do I have in speaking with my beautiful mother?"

"You know you could always make me smile. I love you so much Son. Anyway, I called you because I just received a call from the County Hospital. Your father has been admitted."

"What?"

"I don't know all of the particulars. Your father hasn't been feeling well. He tried to hide it from me but I know my husband and he hasn't been himself for a while. But, he didn't want me to worry so he never complained."

"So why is he in the hospital?"

"I just told you that I don't know. I'm on my way now. I just called your sister and left a voice message. I wanted to call you two before I left for the hospital. As soon as I find out additional information, I'll call you and let you know. Remember Son, I love you."

"I love you too Ummi. I'll make du'a that everything will be fine with Abi."

"In shaa Allah (if it's the will of Allah)."

"In shaa Allah."

Areebah disconnected the phone; went to the car; and drove to the hospital. Her thoughts raced all over the place. She prayed this wasn't anything serious. Up until the past year, he was a healthy man. He always made sure of that. She wondered what was so bad that he had to be hospitalized.

She arrived at the hospital quicker than anticipated. She parked in the parking garage so that she could have more time to her thoughts. Walking from the parking garage to the lobby of the hospital, she pulled on her blue and gray tunic and gray hijab, head covering, a few times. Just as she arrived at the revolving doors of the hospital, she entered the door. She walked up to the security desk and in a soft voice inquired about her husband.

"Hello, I'm here to see Murad Abdul Wali. He's in room 1122."

"I'm sorry Ma'am, I can barely hear you. Will you please speak up," the security officer said.

"Yes, I'm here to see Murad Abdul Wali. He's in room 1122."

"Yes Ma'am. May I please have your driver's license?"

After looking at her driver's license, the

security guard gave her a visitor's pass with the room number written on it along with directions to the room. She headed to the elevators and pressed eleven. The elevator ascended and arrived at the floor in less than a minute. She walked down the hall and heard beeps and dings. Clutching her purse, she entered Murad's room.

"As salaamu alaikum."

"Wa laikum mus salaam. I must look horrible all hooked up to these tubes and machines."

As Areebah walked further into the room, her eyes watered. The closer she got to him, teardrops as large as a raindrop on a spring day flowed down her eyes.

"Yes you do," she said.

"Don't cry, Baby; I love you. We must trust and believe in the qadr (divine will) of Allah, glorified and exalted."

"Just this morning you looked well. I knew you were in pain, but I never expected to see you like this. What did the doctor say? What's the problem?"

"I'm still waiting for him to see me. I haven't heard anything about the results."

"I knew my ears were burning," Dr. Chen said entering Murad's room.

"Dr. Chen, this is my wife."

"Nice to meet you Mrs. Wali."

"I'm sure it would be better under different circumstances; but, nice to meet you too Dr. Chen."

"Well Doc, what are the results?"

"Mr. Wali, would you like to speak with me in private or is it okay to speak with your wife here?"

"You can speak with my wife here."

"Okay, after reviewing the results of the tests and conferencing with my team, the diagnosis is Stage 4 Pancreatic Cancer."

"Pancreatic Cancer? Stage 4! What does that mean Doctor?" Areebah said.

Murad reached out and clasped his hand with Areebah's. All of a sudden, a long exhale exited from him. After a few moments of silence he spoke.

"Doctor, before coming here I researched some of my symptoms. I was afraid this would be the diagnosis."

Dr. Chen sighed and waited for Areebah and Murad to digest the information they just heard.

"Areebah, Baby. I know this is difficult for you to hear," Murad said as he let go of her hand and squeezed her shoulder while motioning for her to have a seat on the bed with him.

The tears started to flow again. Areebah couldn't believe what she was hearing. She wondered how Murad could be so calm with the news they just heard. How can she live life without him she wondered?

"Please take these tissues and wipe your eyes. Right now I need you to make du'a for me, no, for us."

As Areebah turned to face Dr. Chen, it took her a few seconds to find the right words. She glanced around the room, at Murad, and then back at Dr. Chen.

"But Doctor Chen, how could he have pancreatic cancer? He eats all organic and halal foods. He is an avid athlete and he never smoked nor drank."

Looking for the right words to say, Dr. Chen opened Murad's chart and reread the contents. He looked up and just as he was about to speak, Areebah showered him with a slew of questions.

"Is there anything that we can do to kill the cancer cells?" She said grasping for straws.

Dr. Chen looked at Areebah and averted his gaze. He looked up again and saw her hands tremble as she bit her bottom lip. Because of the myriad of questions Areebah was asking regarding a cure for the cancer, Dr. Chen turned and spoke to Areebah.

"As I stated earlier, it is Stage 4. What that means is the cancer is located in more than one region of the body. Because of that, it is incurable. Also, pancreatic cancer is one cancer that has a poor prognosis regardless of when it is diagnosed."

"What is the prognosis Doctor?" She said.

"Six weeks."

"Six weeks? La hawla quwatta wa illah billahi (there's no power or might greater than Allah," Murad said feeling like he was just gut punched.

"Murad, we'll make du'a and we will start juicing more while you take chemotherapy and radiation, maybe a miracle will happen, you may be cured," Areebah said as she tried to find a silver bullet that will kill the cancer and let Murad feel much better.

"Mrs. Wali, I have no doubt in the power of prayer and miracles; however, I will let you know that chemotherapy and radiation may only prolong his life for an additional week or two. Also, the side effects of these treatments are very harsh."

"Doctor Chen, if I take the chemo, am I guaranteed to live the additional week or two?"

"No, I cannot make any guarantees."

"Then I want to go home and live my life without the harsh side effects."

Areebah spun around and stared at Murad with her mouth agape. As the shock wore off, she asked him if he was sure. Her head shook from left to right as he repeated his wishes. After a few moments, she stood up and walked away from the hospital bed.

"Areebah, come here, I need a hug," Murad said.

As she turned back and walked towards his bed, an uncontrollable sob took over.

"Don't cry, Baby," Murad said as tears formed in his eyes.

"I know this was all unexpected and too hard for you to handle; but you know I love you and I don't want to see you cry. So please My Love, let's go home so we can spend the rest of the time I have together at home rather than in the hospital. "

Murad sat up in the bed and turned towards Dr. Chen. He ignored the pain he felt as he began planning for the remainder of his life with his wife. He asked Dr. Chen to prepare him for discharge so he could leave the hospital. Dr. Chen complied; walked out of the door; and headed towards the nurses' station."

"Are you sure you want to leave now?" Areebah said as she shifted from leg to leg after Dr. Chen left the room.

"As I said when Dr. Chen was in here, I don't want to spend the remainder of my life in the hospital. I want us to go home and spend time loving each other."

"I love you too, but I just cannot imagine my life without you," Areebah said as she glanced from the television on the wall to the nurses walking out in the hallway.

"Remember Areebah, Allah doesn't take something from you without replacing it with something better," Murad said in an easygoing manner.

Dr. Chen entered the room and let them know that the release papers would be there soon. He explained to Murad that if he felt any pain or discomfort to contact him. Fifteen minutes later, the nurse walked in the door with the release papers.

"Okay Mr. Wali, here are your release papers. I will have to escort you downstairs and to the curb so you can get in the car with your wife," the nurse said.

Areebah stood up and headed towards the door. Her mind was racing on finding second and third opinions. Just as she turned to exit the hospital room, Murad disrupted her thoughts.

"Don't forget my items over there," Murad said as he ignored the piercing pain he felt each time he spoke.

After grabbing Murad's items, Areebah headed towards the parking garage to get her car. She still couldn't wrap her head around Stage 4 Pancreatic Cancer. While walking she decided to call Sahlah.

"As salaamu alaikum Binti (my daughter)," Areebah said.

"Wa laikum mus salaam Ummi. What's wrong? Why are you crying?"

"I'm just leaving your dad's hospital room where we just met with the doctor. I'm on my way to the car so I can take him home."

"Did you say you just met with the doctor? I can't hear you clearly. Are you sure you're alright?"

"No, I'm not okay. Your father was diagnosed with Stage 4 Pancreatic Cancer."

"SubhanAllah (glory to Allah). Stage 4 Cancer? How did he get it? How long has he had it? Did the doctor give a prognosis?"

"I don't know. They can't explain how the cancer appeared. He said…" Areebah couldn't continue. Without warning the urge to throw the phone against the wall crept in her mind.

"Ummi, call me when you get home. You don't need to be stressed while driving. Call me as soon as you arrive home."

As Areebah walked outside, she saw a huge, ominous mushroom cloud hovering above the hospital and parking garage. As she walked to the garage, the weather outside and the people she passed while walking to her car echoed her feelings.

Two

If she accuses me one more time of anything other than loving her, I'm going to blow a gasket, Frankie thought to himself.

"I saw you looking at the lady at the beach!" Laurie said.

Frankie looked through her. He couldn't believe this conversation was starting again.

"Look Baby, like I told you before, there's no one for me except for you. We've been together for thirty years and married for twenty-eight. I love you and don't want any other woman."

Just as Laurie was about to respond Frankie's phone rang. After glancing at the phone he looked up at Laurie and refused the call. What she didn't know was that he was receiving a lot of unsolicited calls and forgot to install an app to block unwanted calls. However, for the past three months, Laurie's insecurities increased tenfold whenever, his phone rang or a notification of a text appeared.

"Go ahead and answer the phone. Who is it? Stephanie?" Laurie said as her eyes shot daggers at Frankie.

"What? Why would Stephanie be calling me?"

"I'm sure she has a question about work. Isn't that why they all call you?"

"Laurie, it really gets tiring when month after month you accuse me of being with someone or wanting someone else. Is there something you want to tell me? Are you projecting?"

"Don't you dare try to turn this around on me; I'm neither dumb nor blind."

"All I'm saying is that there hasn't been anyone but you for the past thirty years. I don't want anyone but you. In fact, I look forward to us growing old together."

Frankie stood up and walked towards Laurie. He grasped her hand and cradled it in his.

He looked into her amber eyes; moved close to her right ear and whispered, "Laurie, I'm tired of this conversation. It hurts me more than you can imagine. Please, can we forget it? As a matter of fact, knowing that you've been on edge lately, I decided to book a mini vacation for us."

Laurie gazed back into his light brown eyes and gasped. As he whispered in her ear, her mouth closed in slow motion with each word. Tears formed at the corner of her eyes while her lips trembled as she spoke.

"Frankie, I didn't realize that I was hurting you."

All of a sudden she began breathing deeper and more rapid than usual. Frankie rushed over to her because she looked like she was about to pass out. He whispered in her ear to practice the breathing exercises the doctors taught her when she went to the emergency room. The first time this happened, he didn't know what to do. When he thought back on it, he chuckled. He was like a chicken running around with its head chopped off.

However, after it happened with more frequency, the doctor let them know that this was caused by emotional stress. She wrote a referral for Laurie to see a psychologist. Since the breathing exercises helped, she decided that she didn't need to see a psychologist. But, every time she had an episode, Frankie found a way to broach the subject.

"Alright Laurie, sit down and cover your mouth. Breathe from your left nostril."

"Frankie…I…I…I'm…"

"Don't talk right now Baby. I need you to listen to me. Cover your mouth and breathe from your left nostril and then your right nostril."

Frankie went to get a bottle of water because usually after these episodes Laurie was parched when her breathing returned to normal. He never understood why she refused to see the psychologist. It was obvious that there was something psychologically wrong. It's the same dance month after month, year after year. To top it off, it was always over the same foolishness. Not wanting to cause friction in his household, Frankie did all he could to avoid suspicion by Laurie. Nonetheless, she always found something to accuse him of.

"Laurie, have you contacted that psychologist yet?"

"It's nothing wrong with me Frankie. I just allowed myself to get a little excited. I don't need to see a psychologist."

"The last time you had an episode and we took you to the doctor; she suggested you see the psychologist."

"Why are we still talking about this? I don't need to see a shrink. There's nothing wrong with me."

"There's nothing wrong with seeing a psychologist either. Maybe it can help you get away from the foolish thought that I'm cheating or involved with someone else."

"Now you're trying to take my hyperventilation to cover up your relationships with other women."

"Laurie, I told you over and over that there are no other women. However, I feel it's best for you to at least see the psychologist once."

"You know what Frankie? I'm thankful that you helped me get my breath back; however, I don't want to hear any more talk about me seeing a psychologist."

Frankie decided to leave the conversation for

another time. He wanted to get their emotions on a more positive and upbeat fashion. Walking over to Laurie, Frankie caressed her shoulder and kissed the nape of her neck. She softened in his hands. He guided her to the bed and they were engulfed with passion for one another.

Three

The next day, Laurie decided to surprise Frankie for lunch at his office even though she still felt insecure. After the previous night coupled with the idea of them going on a mini vacation all the thoughts of other women with Frankie exited her mind.

Laurie walked up to Frankie's office building and her breathing became labored. She covered her mouth and breathed from one nostril to the next as she approached the front door. She pushed the heavy glass door of the office building open and looked around. The music in the foyer was soft classic rock and the cream marble floors shined as if they were just waxed. The art pieces that hung on the walls complemented the light blue walls. There were remarkable changes since the last time she was there. She wondered why he never mentioned them to her.

Laurie continued her stride taking in the well-decorated entry as various thoughts ran through her mind on how she would invite Frankie to lunch while hinting at the new decorations and why he failed to mention it to her. As she crossed in front of the desk, the faces of the secretary and receptionist soured in an instant. They never liked her; a problem Laurie had all her life with most women and girls. Even in her forties, Laurie maintained a well-toned physique, creamy caramel skin, and a head full of thick, black hair which she kept in a stylish asymmetric bob layered with the longer hair hanging from the left.

She walked with an air of sophistication and superiority at once. As she approached the desk her stroll slowed down. Preparing to offer a fake smile and courteous greeting to the women, Laurie spoke to the women.

"Good afternoon Ladies," Laurie said, to the receptionist and secretary who sat with twisted grins as their arms folded over their chests the moment they made eye contact, "is Frankie–"

Just as Laurie was about to ask for her husband, he and a female colleague walked into the front office shoving each other in a playful fashion and grabbing at one other; stunned, Laurie's mouth dropped as she glared in their direction. What she saw made her light headed as her breathing got deeper and faster. She tried to use the breathing techniques but to no avail. Although she didn't want to cause a scene at his job, he needed to explain what was going on between him and that woman before she exploded.

Just as Laurie was about to say something, Frankie saw Laurie's face turning red although her skin was a creamy peanut butter brown. He stopped dead in his tracks and rushed towards her. Just as she was about to faint, she regained her composure and pushed away from him.

"Laurie, this is Elise our new trainer," he said, avoiding a gaze from either of the women realizing that Laurie is going to be back to beating that same dead horse.

Elise held her hand out to shake Laurie's hand. Against her better judgment, Laurie shook her hand with the limpness of a wet noodle. Frankie saw her chest heave in and out. Although he wanted to reach out and help his wife, he knew now was not the time. After glaring at the three women for an eternity, or at least sixty seconds, Laurie turned on her heels and rushed out the office and into the parking lot. Close on her heels, Frankie called to her.

"Laurie, slow down."

Catching up to her, he reached out to grab Laurie but she recoiled.

"I knew there was something going on between you and someone in your office," she said in a careful, controlled tone while backing away from him.

Frankie was silent and refused to make eye contact. He was not ready to have this conversation again, not here.

"If there is nothing going on, what did I walk in on?" She continued as if his silence was the proof she was searching for.

Frankie remained silent but she didn't ease up on him. She stared him square in the eyes daring him to speak. While staring at him, she raised her hand to cover her mouth and breathe from one nostril to the other. Her skin moistened and her chest began heaving.

"All you saw were two coworkers walking into the office," he said finding his voice as she tried to regulate her breath.

"You touch and play with all of your coworkers?"

Hot with anger, Laurie walked towards her car. She gripped her car keys between her fingers allowing the jagged ends to peek through the slits of her fingers; in a split second, she wished she could jab him with them.

"I came here to surprise you. I guess I was the one surprised."

He stopped next to her car door, leaned in, and spoke in a soft tone, "Let's go to lunch and discuss this."

"No," Laurie said flailing her arms so he wouldn't get close to her, "go to lunch with Elise. Clearly I interrupted your 'work day'."

He stepped back and sputtered but coherent words never left his lips. He reached out to touch Laurie; but, each time he did, she flinched and recoiled as if they were strangers.

"I'm going out by myself," she said, breaking the silence. "I need a drink."

"A drink?" Frankie said as a bile taste rose from his throat. "When did you start drinking again?"

"When did you start caring?"

"That's not fair Laurie," he said keeping his voice low as he spoke through clenched teeth. "You're jumping to conclusions and I've told you time and again that I am not having an affair with anyone. It's you I love and you alone."

"Yes, you've told me time and again. But, time and again while we're together you're either checking your messages or having cryptic conversations on the phone."

"Don't you think it's possible that I'm reading books on the phone? Just because I check the texts doesn't mean anything."

"But doesn't it?"

"Why are you overreacting?"

"Overreacting! How would you feel if you walked into my job and I was playing with a male coworker? When were you going to tell me the décor of the office changed? It looks more like a woman's touch."

"Listen Laurie, although I have a high position here, the décor of the building is not up to me.

And if you must know, the company hired an interior designer. I can understand how you came to the conclusion that Elise and I may have something going on, but there is nothing happening there. I do hope you believe me. But, you're right, I would be angry if I saw something like that. Now that you put it that way, I really understand."

With a long roll of her eyes, Laurie snickered. "I have to go, Frankie. You and your girlfriend can continue playing with each other. I'll see you at home."

Laurie turned before tears fell from her eyes. Remembering that tissue was in the glove compartment, she hurried into the car and snatched the tissue to stop the lone tear from falling. Although she didn't want to drink, this situation moved her closer to that craving. Thirty years since her last drink and one afternoon mishap had her on the brink of drinking. Right after Frankie proposed, he asked her to stop drinking and she did.

Although she wasn't an alcoholic, Laurie often drank too much and became belligerent. So it was not an unreasonable request. Nevertheless, at this moment, she craved a strong drink. The ongoing feeling of Frankie's possible infidelity took her nerves to another level these past few months. A good, strong drink would be the remedy to calm her nerves.

Although the cravings were strong, she

decided to go home. She didn't want her children to see her drunk. They only know her as a loving mother. She refused to let what happened today ruin her sobriety.

Four

Areebah and Murad rode home from the hospital in silence. From time to time, she glanced in his direction. She wanted to reach out and touch him and make everything better. But she knew that wasn't happening.

"Pancreatic Cancer, I don't believe it. I just don't believe it. Let's get a second opinion," Areebah said as she shook her head with vigor.

"Areebah, Baby. I don't want a second opinion. I trust Dr. Chen and although I haven't told you, I've been researching my symptoms and pancreatic cancer came up each time. In shaa Allah, we will make sure to spend as much time together as well as work on the necessary documentation in order to get everything in order for when I die. That way, you will know the next step to take."

"Why are you just accepting it? Why not seek a second opinion?"

"Areebah, you must listen to me."

She twirled the edges of her hijab – head covering - while checking the side and rear mirrors as she drove.

"Areebah?" Murad said trying to get her to listen to him.

"Areebah, I've not felt well for about a year. We really can't say that we believe in Allah and the last day and when we hear something we don't like we begin to question the qadr (divine will). I trust and believe that this is the qadr of Allah and we can use this time to make sure that you are okay after I die. I can also use this time to improve my ibadah (worship). I need your help with that."

"But why did you let me continue making plans to go to Dubai?" Areebah said trying to not let tears fall as her voice shook in concern.

"Although I was pretty sure what the illness was, I prayed that it wasn't and I did not want to unnecessarily worry you. Please dry your eyes, Allah will not take anything away from you without giving you something better."

"But I don't want something better, I want you."

"Are you again questioning Allah's qadr?"

"Why do you keep attacking my iman (faith)? Of course I believe in the qadr of Allah. But there is a hadith (doings, sayings, approvals of Prophet Muhammad, peace be upon him) that states that you are to seek a cure if it exists and the only thing there is no cure for is death. So, why aren't you seeking a cure? It's possible that Dr. Chen could be wrong."

"Areebah, I need you to listen to me. I've been feeling progressively worse. I do not want to go through chemotherapy or radiation, especially if they may only give me an additional two weeks of life but with so many bad side effects."

"Okay," she said as she still planned to check for additional information.

"Well, we're home. Let me help you out of the car."

"I'm not dead yet! I can get out of the car."

Areebah's mouth opened and then closed. She decided against saying anything. Instead, she headed into the house. As she entered the house, she turned and told him, "I'll be there in a few moments; I told Sahlah I'll call her when we returned."

She walked into the office, as soon as she shut the door, tears rushed like water leaves a geyser. Knowing that she had to accept the qadr of Allah and everyone had to die, Areebah decided to use this time to spend as much time as she could with her husband.

After she took time to reflect, she realized that Murad wouldn't leave her destitute. However, what she didn't know was how her life will be without him. Right now she just wanted to cry. No, she needed to cry. Before she called Sahlah, she decided to lock the door and turn on one of her favorite artist. At this time she just wanted to hear the sultry singer sing her favorite song.

The music coming from the office was loud and she could care less. She would rather he heard the loud music than her loud sobbing. She remembered just five years ago Murad's father died of lung cancer and three years before that his mother died of breast cancer. Boy how she hated cancer! As one of her friends on social media used to say F*ck cancer!

Five

I hate seeing Areebah so sad. I know she loves me and we planned to spend the rest of our lives together. In reality, I am living up to my side of the bargain. I am spending the rest of my life with her. I want her to be okay and not be too sad. Mourning is fine, but sometimes she goes a little overboard with her sadness. In shaa Allah, I'll have six weeks to help her understand this transition I'm going through.

I know she's in that office playing the music loud so I can't hear her crying. There have only been a few times that she blasted music and each time it was because I made her sad. I didn't want to sadden her anymore. Maa shaa Allah (it's Allah's will). May Allah subhana wa ta'ala make it easy for her.

Murad walked into the office and peered over at Areebah and didn't know what to say.

"I want Imam Rashid to officiate my janazah," he decided to share.

"I still can't believe that you're discussing

this," Areebah said wishing she could put her fingers in her ears so she didn't have to hear him making plans for death.

"My will is in the safe with the rest of the important papers such as the insurance papers and Social Security information."

"Would you like to go out to eat?"

"I have a janazah kit on the top shelf in the closet."

"I told Sahlah and Baqir they don't need to come here yet."

"Areebah, are you ignoring what I'm saying?"

"I don't want to believe that you are dying."

"If we don't plan now, when the time comes, you will be unprepared."

"Okay, if we go out to lunch, then when we return, I will listen to your death plans," she said sobbing.

"Please don't start crying again."

"How can I not cry? Do you understand that in a little more than a month, you may not be here any…?"

She could not stand any more of this conversation; tears rolled down her eyes and it became difficult for her to breathe. The more she attempted to stop crying, the more she cried. She rushed to the bathroom and performed wudu – ablution, washing the hands, mouth, face, head, ears, and feet. This cooled her down for a moment as she thought about the impending future.

"I know you want to make sure that I am well taken care of. As my grandmother told you before, you are a man's man. But, tonight I need you to hold me and let me cry. I want to be able to cry why you are here so that when you are gone I can remember lying in your arms crying. Right now I'm being selfish. In shaa Allah, tomorrow I'll be strong for you."

"That's fair. Come here."

"Thank you Murad. I love you and I'm thankful that Allah subhana wa ta'ala is providing me the opportunity to say goodbye to you. In shaa Allah, I'll make du'a for you as long as I live and I will encourage our children and subsequent grandchildren to do the same."

"I love you too Baby. Now rest."

Just as Areebah became comfortable in Murad's arms, he jolted up and out of the bed. If Areebah didn't move, the floor would have been her resting place. Murad rushed into the bathroom and vomited. Areebah was right behind him to check on him.

"Why are you staring at me?" Murad said as he finished vomiting.

"I just want to make sure that you're okay," Areebah said frustrated with his outbursts.

"When I need your help I'll ask. Until that time, let me do what I need to do," Murad said.

Six

As time ticked on, she paced the floor enraged. After replaying the lunchtime debacle in her head over and over, Laurie couldn't understand how Frankie didn't see anything wrong. In addition to his refusal to realize that although he was not interested in the women at his job, they did not keep their feelings towards him a secret. His naiveté was neither attractive nor acceptable.

Oftentimes, Laurie overheard conversations between Frankie and a couple of his coworkers very seldom did the conversations stay on the reason for the calls. Today was the first time she'd seen the interaction between her husband and his coworkers, especially that Elise. It didn't sit well with her; as a matter of fact, just thinking about it made her blood boil.

Dinner time was approaching and Laurie entered the kitchen to begin cooking. As she pulled out the ingredients for dinner, her anger escalated. Banging the pots and pans in the sink and on the stove, slamming the chicken into the sink and washing it roughly as if she was trying to rub its skin off, Laurie could have been arrested for chicken abuse.

Grabbing the largest knife in the drawer, Laurie stabbed into the center of the breast; ripped the leg from the thigh as if there were no tendons holding them together; as she ripped the wing from the breast she pondered over what to do with Frankie. Once the chicken was cut, she shook the seasonings onto the chicken and the powdered seasonings dispersed around the sink. Livid over her own sloppiness, and mind racing over her failing marriage, she grabbed the box of aluminum foil from the kitchen drawer and yanked it from the roll and ripped it from the box. After covering the pan, Laurie threw the chicken into the pan and covered it then slammed the pan into the preheated oven, smacking her careless hand against the inside of the oven.

"Damn," she said wincing in pain from hitting her hand on the top rack inside the oven.

If it wasn't one thing it was another, this was not her day. Her eyes watered as she searched the kitchen for the first aid kit before realizing it was under the kitchen sink. After dressing the burn, she returned to cooking dinner although she was twice as irritable as she was earlier in the day. Just as she was about to prepare rice and vegetables,

Frankie walked in.

"I'm home," he said smiling and laughing with the children.

The urge to drink reared its ugly head as soon as Laurie heard Frankie's voice. How dare he come in here smiling and laughing? She could hear the children rush to their dad asking him about work. She remained in the kitchen and began running her hand under cold water. Something needed to cool her down and the water over the burn provided relief. She turned the water off and walked out of the kitchen; passed Frankie and the children; and headed towards the front door.

"Where are you going?" Frankie said as he and the children watched her leave the kitchen.

"Out!"

Frankie's black, bushy eyebrows drew close together. His soft brown lips twisted into a frown, giving his chocolatey features a displeased scowl. "Seriously? Where are you going?"

"Don't worry about it. I'll be gone long enough for you to talk and chat with whomever you'd like."

Frankie turned to his children. "Go to your room. I'll call you down when it's time to eat."

Rushing towards their rooms the children whispered under their breaths wondering what was going on. Arguing in front of the children was one thing they agreed not to do. Laurie held off her response to his questions until the children walked up the stairs.

"What do you want, Frankie?"

"Whoa, what's up with the attitude?"

"I'm sick of you," she said picking her purse up from the glass coffee table as she walked across the room towards the front door.

"Laurie, I really don't understand you right now. Why are you tripping?"

"Why am I tripping? Are you serious? I go to your job and you are playing around with a woman. You want me to behave like I didn't see it?"

Frankie rubbed his temples. "Laurie, I understand what you think you saw—"

"What I think I saw?" she released a smug chuckle. "Frankie, I will be back. I cannot be in the house with you right now. The chicken is in the oven. I didn't start the vegetables or rice, you can cook those. I'll be back sooner or later."

Laurie snatched her purse from the table and strutted to the door.

Frankie sighed. "Laurie, instead of you running away from this issue, why don't we meet it head-on and discuss it?"

"Frankie, at this time I do not want to discuss anything with you. So, please finish dinner. I'll be back as soon as I can." She grabbed the door handle, opened it, and stepped outside.

"At least tell me where you are going, Laurie?"

"I'm going to the bar to have a few drinks."

Frankie walked to the sofa and sank into it;

lowered his head; and rubbed his temples. He then looked at Laurie confused. She stared back at Frankie and laughed. Before he could make up another excuse for his deplorable actions, Laurie nodded her head, turned around with a smirk and slammed the door.

On the other side of the door, Laurie leaned against the shut door on the verge of tears. Why am I going out to drink?

Looking around, she turned to grab the doorknob to reenter the house. Rather than get into an altercation she knew she'd lose, she decided to stay away for a while and calm down. Furthermore, she wanted Frankie to suffer as much as she did today after seeing him with Elise, and she knew being away from the house under these conditions would drive him crazy.

Laurie couldn't understand why her husband would cheat on her. Working out was a daily routine and she always ate healthy. Her face was made up to perfection each day and she made sure to engage with him on every level. It befuddled her why he would fathom cheating on her with anyone. Just thinking about what she saw today incensed her even more.

In all reality, she didn't want to drink to make him pay, but for now it was the only way she knew to strike a nerve with Frankie. He hated alcoholics – his stepfather was one. Over thirty years ago she made a promise to herself to not drink any alcoholic beverages. Therefore, she would not drink, but she did plan on staying out for a couple of hours.

While sitting at the bar, Laurie used her cell phone to visit the web to see if she could find information about this Elise woman. Various social media accounts appeared as well as a few legal documents from the county. She found out that Elise was under investigation for the murder of a former coworker's wife. For a brief moment, Laurie considered driving over to Elise's house and giving her a piece of her mind. However, she valued her life and was not interested in going to jail.

Laurie decided to hang out at the bar and enjoy the music while watching people enter and leave the bar, sometimes alone but more times than not with someone they just met before getting drunk. Realizing she'd been gone for a while, Laurie decided to look at her phone. The phone had been muted from the time she arrived at the bar, she was certain she'd receive a phone call from Frankie and she wanted to make him sweat. However, when she looked at the phone not only was there a missed call from her husband; there were fifteen missed calls each and every one from Frankie. Laurie grinned a devilish grin and then checked her voicemails.

"Laurie, Sweetie, I can't wait until you get home," Frankie said.

"Laurie, come home, we need to talk."

"Laurie…enough is enough; you need to get

home right now!"

"Laurie, this is bullshit! You can't just fall of the face of the earth, where are you?

Tired of hearing all of the messages, Laurie deleted the remaining messages. She'll get home in due time.

Turning her attention back to people watching, Laurie tried to forget what she saw at Frankie's job and relieve her jealous anxiety. She looked at her phone one last time and realized there was another set of voicemails. There were five calls from her children. Seeing her children's phone numbers on her caller ID made her realize that the bar was not the place for her to be right now. It was time to head home. She and Frankie would have to discuss things when she got home.

Three hours after leaving the house, Laurie finally returned home exhausted. As she walked into the house and went to the kitchen, to her surprise the kitchen was spotless and a plate with an apology card awaited her on the stove. Seeing the kind gesture, her heart softened. Eager to see what else Frankie had up his sleeve, she walked upstairs to their bedroom. Entering the dim room, she heard old school slow jams fill the room. The song brought back happy memories of their early years together. Soaking in the moment, Laurie averted her gaze across the room and saw her husband lying on the bed. He was under the burgundy sheet and his caramel chiseled chest called to her while the white shorts accentuated his manhood. As his six foot three inch frame laid across the California king bed, Laurie couldn't help but smile. Sauntering over to the bed, she bent down to hug Frankie. She then melted into his arms and kissed him with so much passion and love that the day floated from her mind.

"I'm sorry, baby. Those women really do not mean anything to me. Since I see how much it bothers you, I will limit my interactions with them."

Tears fell down Laurie's eyes. She expected him to yell; give her the silent treatment; or fault her for overreacting, however, these actions made her love him just a little more.

"While you were gone, Laurie, I thought about the mini vacation we discussed the other day."

"That sounds like a good idea. When do you think we should do it?" She said.

"I was thinking tomorrow and stay until the end of the weekend," he said

"That does sound great, but what about the children?" She said.

"Well, Jabari is nineteen and technically that makes him an adult. We can leave them some food and money," he said.

"Sounds great Frankie, let's view some hotels so we can decide where we're going to stay."

"Hotel is already booked."

"Already? You sneaky devil you. I love you Frankie."

Seven

The next day Frankie and Laurie headed out to their rendezvous. He hoped this time away from the children and work would help them get their spark back. Although she said she forgave him, at times she would make comments that were eerily similar to conversations he had either on the phone or while he was on social media. He didn't want to believe that she put spyware on his electronics, but remembering how his father was betrayed by a friend who landed him in prison, he began pulling from his upbringing, which taught him that infiltrators can come from anywhere.

Frankie wanted this time away to be a positive turning point in their relationship. Sitting in an uncomfortable silence, he hoped that they enjoyed themselves. Thirty minutes into the ride,

Laurie turned towards Frankie.

"I really appreciate you planning this time away for us Frankie. I know we've been having problems for a while. I miss how it was. Believe it or not, I'm excited."

Frankie turned towards Laurie and smiled. He first thought this trip was going to be a failure. However, after seeing the smile on her face and hearing the hopefulness in her voice, a sense of relief fell over him.

Fifteen minutes later they turned onto the hotel grounds. There were exquisite manicured bushes shaped like animals and geometric shapes. There are waterfalls and fountains throughout the grounds. Luscious green golfing grounds with small hills and ponds can be seen for miles.

"Look at the landscape of this place. I expected it to be beautiful, but the landscape leaves me breathless," Laurie said with giddiness as she rolled the windows down to take pictures of the landscape with her phone.

"I'm glad you like it Baby, just wait until you get inside," he said, feeling on top of the world.

He pulled into the valet parking area, exited the car, walked around to open Laurie's door. Leaving the car with the valet attendant, he escorted Laurie into the hotel.

"Frankie, what a breathtaking view, the waterfalls are breathtaking. Look at the exotic fish and ducks in the water. I can just imagine what the rooms look like," she said as she laced her arm through his and nestled closely to him.

"Laurie, I know how much you love waterfalls, so when I saw this hotel online, I knew this was the place for you; no, for us. I've caused so much grief for you recently and I want you to know how much I love and appreciate you. Take your time and enjoy the ambiance while I check in and get our keys." He walked away leaving Laurie to take in the spectacular view.

"Come on Baby," Frankie said, as he walked up to Laurie.

Startled out of her thoughts, Laurie turned around and smiled. She reached out and embraced him and held him tight. Their lips locked and she melted into his arms; he returned the embrace and pulled her closer. What a great start, he thought as he continued tasting her and feeling her soft body against his.

"Thank you again for this. I'm looking forward to this weekend. I haven't seen the room yet, but if this is any measure of the room, I am sure to be impressed."

"I aim to please." His eyes glowed with excitement. "We're in Room 209," Frankie said.

They left the main area of the hotel and walked to the elevators. As soon as the elevator doors opened, they stepped in holding each other's hand while gazing into each other's eyes.

As they exited the elevator, they rushed from the elevator to the room. Thinking about the kiss,

Frankie opened the door and ushered Laurie into the room. As soon as she entered the room, her eyes watered and she rushed into his arms. Knowing the reaction would be priceless, just as she turned he clicked the photo with his camera.

Hand over her mouth, Laurie shrieked, and said, "Frankie, the heart shaped bed is beautiful. How did you get the rose petals on the bed?"

She then turned her attention to the bathroom, "Wow, A heart-shaped hot tub too? Thank you, Frankie. You always knew how to make me feel special."

"You outdid yourself. Where did you find this place? Have you been here before?"

Frankie shook his head. "I searched the web for a hotel in the area and when I saw this one and viewed the pictures, I knew you would like this one. What about the view, isn't it beautiful?"

Laurie sauntered to the window that overlooked the city's skyline. Looking out the window, she suddenly became quiet.

Baffled by her rapid change of emotions, Frankie walked over to the window and hugged his wife. "Why are you crying, baby? You don't like the room?"

"I love the room. I love the entire hotel," she said releasing a dejected sigh. "I'm crying because I didn't expect anything this grand. I know we've been having hard times lately, but this hotel room – no, this entire weekend lets me know you love me and listen to my feelings."

Frankie took her by the hand and brought Laurie to the bed and began disrobing her. With their bodies feeling the warmth of the other, their lips locked and all negative tension between them left.

Frankie reached behind the bedpost and handed her a shiny red gift bag decorated with a heart and lace. Tears welled in her eyes as she opened the bag. Laurie emptied the contents of the bag on the bed and a bright cherry satin slip and a pair of red marabou fur and clear slipper heels tumbled out. Followed by the fragrance Frankie loved the most on her, mango allusion body care collection, Laurie was speechless.

"If you keep treating me like this," she said, as she embraced Frankie again, "we will have to get away more often."

"That's my intent."

"I'm going to enjoy the tub, would you like to join me?" Laurie said, as she sashayed towards the bathroom.

"No, you go enjoy yourself. I know how you like to soak in the tub and read. This is time for you to enjoy yourself. We'll bathe again later after we eat."

While Laurie bathed, Frankie decided to do a little channel surfing. While he was flipping through channels, his phone rang.

Who is calling me? I told everyone not to bother me unless it's an emergency, he thought to himself.

Frankie looked at his phone and saw the call was from his sister.

He pressed the mute button on the remote and laid back on the bed, staring at the ceiling. "Hello?"

"Hey Frankie," Felicia said.

"What's up, Felicia?"

"It's Mom," she said with a quiver in her voice.

Frankie paused. He wasn't used to his sister calling sounding so distressed. Sitting upright in the chair, Frankie felt a knot form in his gut. "What about mom?"

"She's in the hospital–"

"For what?"

His sister sniffled and took in a deep breath before speaking. "We're not sure," she said, sniffling once again. The shakiness in her voice indicated Felicia was on the verge of tears. "At this time, she's unresponsive."

"Unresponsive?" They both quieted for a brief moment. "What do you need from me?

"You need to get here as soon as you can."

Frankie thought of Laurie. As soon as he tried to make amends with his wife a family emergency occurred. Frankie and Laurie had to cut their time at the hotel short. There was nothing he could do about it, she'd have to understand.

"I'll try to catch the next flight out, Felicia," Frankie said. Looking up, he spotted Laurie fresh out of the hot tub posted against the frame of the bathroom doorway, wrapped in a white towel.

"Laurie, I just got off the phone with Felicia."

Laurie just stared at Frankie.

"She said mom was rushed to the hospital and she's unresponsive."

"So, why did she call you?"

"I just told you my mother was unresponsive. Why do you think she called me?"

"I'm just saying. We just reconnected and are rebuilding our relationship. Couldn't she wait a couple of days?"

"Are you serious Laurie? My mother is in the hospital unresponsive and you want my sister to wait a couple of days before contacting me? What has gotten into you?"

"Frankie, you know what? I didn't mean to be callous. But, damn! We're just getting right."

"Look Laurie, it's just Felicia and I. If my mother is unresponsive, I am going to see her and it is not up for discussion."

"Frankie, you're right. I was being selfish because there's been a lot of tension between us lately and I thought this would bring us back on track."

"Laurie, as much as I love you, I must go and see about my mother. Going to see about her is not going to take away from what I had planned for the two of us. If I have to spend the remainder of my life proving to you how much I love you, I will. But at this time we need to pack and I'm going to the front office to see if they can give me a rain check."

"Okay Frankie. But before you go downstairs, I want to let you know that I know this weekend was to help us eliminate strain on our marriage and you ensured me that you are not involved with anyone. But, it is difficult for me to believe it. Please, when you go to Philly think of me and try not to see any old friends," Laurie said.

"Laurie, as I've told you before, there is nothing between me and anyone other than you. I know you find it hard to believe, however, I am not nor have I ever lied to you, ever," Frankie was growing sick of this conversation and no matter what he told Laurie, she refused to believe him.

"I'm going to the front office and I'll be right back. Please pack up so we can check out and leave. I need to see what the problem with my mother is."

Eight

Frankie arrived in Philadelphia at two in the morning; picked up his rental car; then headed to the hotel. The extra-large vases with flowers and various art pieces welcomed him into the hotel. After checking in he went up to his room. The comfort of the hotel room enveloped him. The bed was so comfortable that as soon as his head hit the pillow he fell asleep.

A few hours later, the combination of the sun shining on his face and the shrilling sound of the phone ringing nonstop awakened him. When he turned over to answer the phone, the ringing stopped. Now that he was wide awake, he looked at his phone and saw thirty missed calls. Just as he was about to check who called so many times, the phone rang once again.

"Hello," Frankie said, answering the phone. Sleep coated his voice making it deeper than usual.

"Hey Baby, how was your flight?"

"It was good. It was difficult for me to sleep last night. You know I only get a good night's sleep when you're in bed beside me," Frankie said.

"I was just thinking that same thing," replied Laurie

"Great minds…"

They both laughed. Often they had similar thoughts and they always said the beginning of the phrase, "Great minds think alike."

"Have you seen your mom yet?"

"Not yet, believe it or not, I'm just waking up."

"I believe it, I called you so many times and there was no answer."

"Why so many times?"

"I was just concerned and needed to hear your voice. I need your touch. I miss you Baby."

"I miss you too. Hopefully it's nothing serious with my mom and I'll be back sooner than later."

"Okay, well go see your mother and sister and hurry back."

After disconnecting the phone, Frankie showered and went to the valet to retrieve his car. Twenty minutes later, Frankie pulled up to the hospital. He left his car in the care of the valet attendant and headed to the security desk so he could get to see his mother.

"Hello, I am here to see Inez Williams."

"Yes sir, may I please see your driver's license?"

Looking through his wallet, Frankie fished his driver's license out and handed it to the security guard. After handing it to her, she inspected the front and back of the license. He didn't understand what the problem was.

"Are you having problems with my driver's license?" He said becoming frustrated.

"I'm just doing my job," said the security guard glaring at him.

"And it requires you to look at it three times and stare at me?" He massaged his temples as he glanced at the clock waiting for her to return his driver's license.

"Inez Williams?" she said so soft he had to strain to hear as she prepared his visitor's badge.

"Yes," Frankie replied just wanting his driver's license back so he can go see his mother. He walked to the elevator and entered it. Less than a minute later he was on the floor where his mother was. Anxiety crept into his mind as he slowed his pace.

Although he and his mother spoke often on the phone, years passed since he saw her. The door opened and Frankie took a deep, pained breath and started down the hall towards his mother's room. All of a sudden he wished he spent more time with his mother rather than taking multiple vacations around the world.

Not paying attention to his surroundings, he

looked up and realized he was in front of his mother's room. Staring down at his feet, he entered the room, tears rushing down his face. When he turned the corner, his mother stared at him surprised to see him standing at her door.

"Frankie?" Inez said.

"I'm sorry they called you here," she continued.

"Sorry? Mom, I've neglected you between my work and vacations. What do you have to be sorry for?"

Frankie bent down and gave his mother a hug. She felt frail and weak since the last time he saw her. His eyes welled up with tears as he sat beside her.

Inez sat up and looked Frankie in the eyes, "You haven't neglected me. I encouraged you to take your family to those trips around the world. As a matter of fact, although I'm happy that you are here, this old bird isn't going anywhere anytime soon."

"But Felicia told me that you weren't doing so well and I needed to get here as soon as possible," he said in an unsteady voice.

"At the time she found me, it was a little touch and go. However, I just spoke with the doctor and I'm fine. I'll be going home in a couple of days."

"Well, mom, that's good news. But, did they say what caused you to fall and become unresponsive?"

"No, they really don't have any answers. However, after all of the tests they performed on me, nothing conclusive appeared. They just want me to not climb and to see my doctor more frequent."

"And they're sending you home so soon? Even at your age, they aren't concerned?"

"My age? Come on Frankie, I'm not that old."

"Mom, you're seventy-two. Although you may not feel old, there is still something going on there."

"It is possible that they're letting me out because I don't have good insurance. However, I do feel much better and I think everything will be okay."

"Okay, well, I'm going to call Laurie and let her know you're fine. She was concerned about you."

"Great, give her my love and tell her and the kids not to worry."

Frankie walked out into the hall to call Laurie. The phone went straight to voicemail so he tried again.

"She didn't answer," Frankie said, as he reentered his mother's room. "I'll try again after I leave. So, mom, what's been happening in the City of Brotherly Love and Sisterly Affection?"

"Nothing and everything, you know how that is. By the way, I was talking to Kashifah the other day. Do you remember Kashifah?"

Just the sound of the name brought Frankie

back to his teen years. Kashifah and Inez were friends and comrades in the Black Panther Party of Philadelphia. After the party disbanded, they remained friends for a while. Kashifah had a daughter named Areebah. Frankie and Areebah were inseparable; everyone thought they would get married.

"Yes, mom, of course I remember Kashifah. How are she and Shafaat?"

"They're doing just fine. However, Areebah's husband is not doing well. He has pancreatic cancer and was given six weeks to live."

"Six weeks," Frankie stood up and looked out the window as he took time to digest the news he just heard. He couldn't imagine how he would feel if he was told he had six weeks to live. He struggled to find the right words.

"How is Areebah handling this news?" Frankie said not knowing what else to say.

"It's difficult for her. But, you know she's Muslim and Kashifah said she is leaving it in Allah's hands."

He paced back and forth, "I'll be right back Mom. I'm going to try Laurie again."

Frankie walked to the visitors' waiting room to call Laurie again. The room had two televisions in it and one was blaring. He walked over and turned down the volume. He then called Laurie again.

He called her phone three more times. While waiting for her to answer, his thoughts drifted to

Areebah. He wondered if she was on social media. It would be great to chat with her. He brushed that thought out of his mind. Laurie was already suspicious of the women at work; he didn't want to give her more fuel for the fire.

Frankie went back into his mother's room and saw her resting. He walked to the chair and sat down making sure not to disturb her. Curiosity took the best of him and he typed Areebah's name in the search of the social media website. After clicking search, a picture of the most beautiful woman appeared. Unmistakably, it was Areebah. Her almond shaped, cognac brown eyes accented her brown skin that rivals coffee when it's mixed with a little too much creamer.

She had on the most beautiful wine-red with black flowery designed headscarf and the smile that melted every man that met her heart. Frankie exited the app from his phone so temptation wouldn't takeover. He walked back to his mother's room to check on her. She was still resting.

Walking back to the waiting room, he decided to sit down and watch a little television. He then tried Laurie once again. But again there was no answer. Instead of waiting for her to return his call, he decided to call Jabari, his eldest son living at home.

"Hello Dad," Jabari answered.

"Hey Jabari, where's your mom?"

"She's in the room," Jabari said after a slight

hesitation.

"Why isn't she answering her phone?" Frankie said wondering what the hesitation was about.

After a few moments of silence, Frankie asked the question again through his teeth with forced restraint.

"She's passed out," Jabari said with a slight tremble in his voice.

"Passed out? What do you mean passed out?" Frankie said yelling making an older man sitting in the room jerk his head in Frankie's direction.

"Ever since you left, Mom has been drinking. She hasn't cooked for us and she's been cursing at us whenever she's awake," Jabari said on the brink of crying.

"I'm on my way. I'll be there in the morning. I need you to pick me up from the airport. Don't tell your mom that I'm on my way home."

Anger swept over Frankie. He knew when he and Laurie had the issues with the women at work that she threatened to drink, but she never did. However, for her to get drunk and not take care of the children there's no excuse for that.

Frankie took the time to calm down before returning to his mother's room. He didn't want her to see him upset because although the doctors are allowing her to go home, Franke still wanted her to remain as stress free as possible.

"Well Mom, since you are getting released tomorrow, I'm going to head back home," Frankie said feigning contentment.

"How was Laurie? Did you tell her I'm okay?"

"Laurie's fine. I'm going to talk to her in more detail when I get home."

"Okay Frankie, by the way. It was a pleasure seeing you. I love you Son."

"I love you to Mom," Frankie bent over and kissed his mother on the cheek. He wished he could stay a couple of days more; but he had to get home and get a handle on this.

Nine

"As salaamu alaikum Ummi," Areebah greeted her mother once she answered the phone.

'Wa laikum mus salaam Areebah. How's everything going?"

"Everything's well, Alhamdulillah,"

"What's the matter Sweetie? You sound kind of down."

"Ummi…"

"Yes Sweetie, what's the problem? Is everything okay with the children?"

"Murad...has…"

"Murad has what? Areebah, take your time. What about Murad?"

"A few weeks ago Murad was diagnosed with pancreatic cancer and he's been given six weeks to live."

"SubhanAllah (Glory to Allah)!"

"We're on our way down there now."

Kashifah disconnected the phone and looked at her husband with tears streaming down her face."

"What's wrong Shifa? What was that conversation about?" Areebah's father Shafaat asked as soon as she disconnected the phone.

"Murad was diagnosed with pancreatic cancer and was given six weeks to live."

"Six weeks! La hawla quwatta wa illah billah (There is no power or might greater than Allah)."

"What are we waiting for, we need to get down there and help our baby," Shafaat said while Kashifah already had the suitcases out and was packing the clothes and cosmetics.

"Go online and reserve a car. I cannot imagine what Areebah is going through."

"Shifa, I know you're sad and concerned for Areebah. If I could take the tears and hurt from you and her I would. But, there are some things that are greater than me."

"I know Shaf. Areebah's been telling me that Murad's been feeling bad for a while. But no way would I have imagined cancer."

Kashifah sat on the edge of the bed winded. The call she received from Areebah was the last thing she expected. Areebah and Murad were just beginning to spend time together without children and then this disease attacked him.

After packing their clothes and putting them in the car, Kashifah and Shafaat headed to Areebah and Murad's house. While Shafaat was driving, Kashifah observed a shimmer of golden sun shaking through the trees. She couldn't fathom the pain and distress her daughter had to endure. The time seemed to go in a blur. Not knowing what to expect when she arrived, Kashifah was in continuous dhikr – remembrance of Allah. That was the only way she could calm herself.

On the other hand, Shafaat was talking to Kashifah about various topics. She replied with an occasional "uh huh" or "yep", but in reality she was not listening to what he was saying. Her mind was on their only child and what lie ahead of her due to her husband's illness. Kashifah wondered why this trip was taking longer than all of the previous times they've taken this trip.

Shafaat stopped for gas and Kashifah stepped out to use the restroom. It seemed like the discussion of cancer was all around her. She looked at the newspapers and the headlines touted how cancer is becoming one of the most diagnosed diseases. She walked into the store and on the television the newscaster was talking about cancer studies. As she entered the restroom she overheard one lady talking to the other about someone being diagnosed with cancer.

After returning back to the car, Kashifah broke down crying. She had so many friends afflicted with that wretched disease. By no means did she ever think her son-in-law would be diagnosed with it. How her baby must be beside herself in grief.

"What's the matter?" Shafaat asked Kashifah as he sat in his seat.

"I'm just so sad about Murad and I'm thinking of how sad Areebah must be."

"You know they both trust and believe in Allah subhana wa ta'ala. I'm sure they're deep in du'a."

"I agree, but we are still human and this must be hurtful."

"Are you questioning the qadr of Allah?"

"Not at all! But, we are human and sadness is acceptable. I have the right to worry about my daughter and her husband."

"But, Allah is in charge of all things."

"And by no means am I saying that He is not. However, I am exercising my right to be sad. Even the Rasullullah, sallahu alaihi wa salaam (Messenger of Allah, may peace be upon him) wept when his son died."

"Maa shaa Allah (It's Allah's will)," Shafaat said.

He really makes me angry when he doesn't allow me to express my feelings. I trust and believe in Allah and I am not questioning His qadr, but I need to express this grief, Kashifah thought to herself.

"Well, we're about thirty minutes away so get yourself together and stop crying."

"Get myself together? Arc you serious?"

"Yes, you should not go in there crying. Let

your daughter know that you are strong."

"Sometimes I think you just don't understand me. But, okay. I'll get myself together," she said sapping with sarcasm which made him turn around and stare at her.

Shafaat and Kashifah arrived at Areebah and Murad's house. Although she was still upset with the dismissive tone of her husband, Kashifah did gain her composure to go see her daughter. She couldn't wait to get inside and hug her daughter. They gathered their items from the car and walked toward the front door; just before they were about to knock on the door, their grandson, Baqir, opened the door.

Kashifah hugged her grandson so tight that he looked to his grandfather for help.

"Let the boy go Kashifah!"

"It's okay Granddad," Baqir said not wanting to offend his grandmother.

"As salaamu alaikum Baqir. How are your mom and dad?"

"They're hanging in there, Jeddah (Grandmom). They're sitting on the back patio. Abi wanted to enjoy the fresh air."

Shafaat, Kashifah, and Baqir headed back to the patio. While walking through the house, Kashifah noticed the hospital bed and walker. Tears formed as soon as she saw these items; however, she remembered what Shafaat told her about having composure so she wiped her eyes. She couldn't wait to get out of the house.

As soon as Kashifah set foot into the patio, Areebah rushed into her mother's arms. Both began to weep and embrace one another.

"Let's go into the kitchen and prepare something for everyone to eat," Areebah said.

"Okay, let's go. We really didn't eat in the last few hours."

"So how are you really doing?" Kashifah asked Areebah once they were away from everyone.

"At first it was really difficult. However, Murad has been my rock. Can you believe it? He's the one dying and he is helping me instead of me helping him."

"He is a good man and he always wanted the best for you. May Allah subhana wa ta'ala make it easy for all of you."

"Ameen."

"Sahlah and Baqir arrived last night. I feel so good having my entire family here."

"Where else would we be?"

"I know. But sometimes I go in the office to cry because Murad is so strong and I don't want him to think I lost my faith."

"I understand Baby. Your father is the same way. He told me to stop crying and accept the qadr of Allah."

"Ummi, sometimes men just don't get it. I guess we are the more emotional gender."

"I thought you were getting food for us," Shafaat said interrupting their conversation.

"It's just about done. Abi, please be kinder to

Ummi. It's hard when one loses, or is about to lose a spouse."

"Areebah, you're right. Thank you for giving this old man naseeha (advice). But seriously, I'm famished. What are we going to eat?" he said trying to break the tension in the room.

"Give us a few more minutes and a delectable feast will be in front of you," Areebah said with a smile.

Areebah was the only one who could soften her father. Shafaat walked back onto the patio as the women began preparing the food. A few minutes later there was a spread with fried snapper, macaroni and tuna salad, spinach, and croissants. They also made some fresh squeezed lemonade and fresh brewed iced tea.

"Alhamdulillah!" Baqir said as he saw his mother and grandmother entering with the food.

"Greedy," Sahlah said teasing her brother.

"Alright you two," Murad said smiling at the camaraderie between his children.

Kashifah stood back and looked at her family. She beamed with pride. Not just because they were together but because they are all striving in the cause of Allah subhana wa ta'ala. Although she was sad on her way to see Areebah and Murad, a sense of sakinah, calm, washed over her. She had tears in her eyes again; however, this time they were tears of contentment.

"Let's clear the area and clean the dishes Areebah," Kashifah said.

"Sahlah and Baqir can do it," Areebah said.

"Let us do it," Kashifah said using her mother voice while placing her hands on her hips.

"Okay Ummi."

They gathered the food, dishes, and glasses and took them to the kitchen. Kashifah made sure everyone was alright and walked into the kitchen.

"What's up Ummi?"

"Do you remember Inez?"

"Frankie's mom?" Areebah said. All of a sudden her heart raced.

"Yes, her."

"Yes I do. What about her?"

"She was in the hospital a few days ago. She told me that Frankie came to visit her and asked about you."

Frankie. I haven't thought about Frankie in decades. I wonder how he's doing, Areebah thought.

"Ummi, why are you telling me this?"

"Inez and I were reminiscing and we always wondered why you two never got together."

"Well Ummi, it is that thing about him not being Muslim."

"Oh yeah, well, Inez tells me he's happily married with eight children. She asked about you. I told her about Murad and his diagnosis of pancreatic cancer."

"Well, it's good that he's happily married. I hope Inez will be okay."

Why would Ummi bring Frankie up? He and I wanted to get married but Abi was always against it. Abi never gave him dawah (invitation to Islam) or anything. I wonder why? Anyway, he's happily married and still not Muslim, Areebah mused.

"Based on what you've been telling me, it seems as if Murad only has days left. As a Muslimah, you can remarry. Maybe Frankie will accept his Shahadah."

"But there's still that thing about him being happily married. Anyway Ummi, I am not thinking of that right now. I am concerned with taking care of my husband."

"Okay, I'll drop it. But Areebah, you're still young. Even if not Frankie, please remember that you don't have to spend the remainder of your life alone."

Areebah thoughts went to Frankie. They spent so much time together as little children and teenagers. Their parents were members of the Black Panther Party of Philadelphia and the children were involved in many activities. She remembered marching with him and singing cadences. They had so much fun together. He was the first boy she kissed. She wondered what he looked like thirty-five years later.

Guilt washed over Areebah for thinking about another man while her husband was in the other room fighting an unbeatable fight. Nevertheless, she still was curious. Even if he wasn't Muslim, she would like to see him one time.

She shook those thoughts away and went to check on her family. She saw everyone standing around Murad. His breathing was belabored. He was having difficulties keeping his eyes open. She heard her father encourage her husband to say, "La illaha il-Allah, Muhammad Dar Rasullullah (there is no god but Allah and Muhammad is the messenger of Allah.)"

She squeezed between her father and Murad. She bent down and kissed him on the lips.

"Oh my Murad, I love you. May Allah subhana wa ta'ala grant you Jennatil Firdaus (the highest heaven). May your grave be spacious; and may Allah subhana wa ta'ala forgive all of your sins."

Tears streaked down Areebah's face. She looked around and everyone was in a somber mood. Since the second week of Murad's diagnosis, she hired a Home Health Aide. There was also a nurse who visited him three times a week. The Home Health Aide, Malika, was very helpful and helped her know what to expect during this illness.

Malika heard the death rattle in Murad's throat and asked the family to step out of the room. Unbeknownst to the family her employer provided her with morphine and instructed her that when it looked as if he was close to death, she was to increase his dosage of morphine so he can pass away in peace.

Areebah asked everyone to leave the room so Malika could assist Murad. She injected him with the morphine and then cleaned his area. She expected him to stop breathing in the next thirty minutes. She told the family that she cleaned him and they can go see him. While they were in the room, she called her employer to let them know that she injected the final dosage of morphine.

"What did you say?" Baqir said frightening Malika. She thought they were all in the room.

"Ummi! Come out here right now! She killed Abi!"

Ten

"Passengers, please buckle your seatbelts. We are experiencing terrible turbulence," the pilot said after about twenty minutes in the air.

Frankie looked out the window and saw dark, water laden, and mountainous clouds. Lightning struck through the clouds. Instead of in a plane, Frankie felt as if he was on a roller coaster but he knew the ground was much further down from the airplane than the roller coaster. Remembering how much Laurie drank prior to their marriage, it was hard for Frankie to see a positive outcome from her drinking.

"Is this plane and weather preparing me for what is waiting for me at home?"

Although the turbulence was bad, the plane arrived a few minutes before scheduled.

"Ding," the speakers from the plane chimed.

"You are now able to turn on your phones; but please remain in your seats until the aircraft comes to a complete stop," the pilot reminded the travelers.

Frankie turned on his phone and saw six missed calls and twenty texts; all from Laurie. Disregarding the messages and texts, he called Jabari to see if he was at the airport yet.

"Yes, I'm in the short-term parking."

"Okay, meet me at the departure gate; I should be there in five minutes."

Rushing through the crowd, Frankie weaved in and out of foot traffic. He couldn't wait to get into the car and have a little peace and quiet. As soon as he walked out the door, he heard his car before he saw it because there was loud, booming music coming from the car. He winced at the sound.

"Hey Dad!" Jabari said as he waved him over to the car with enthusiasm.

"Hey Son," Frankie said.

A few minutes later while driving down the highway, Frankie clasped his hands behind his back. After a couple more minutes, he reached for the volume and turned the volume down.

"Why do you insist on playing this ridiculous music so loud?"

"It's soothing," said Jabari.

Frankie looked at his son and decided to pick his battles. He knew one was brewing at home so he just let it be at this time. Fifteen minutes into the drive, he turned to Jabari and saw his jaw clenched. After looking further, he also saw a lone tear in the corner of his eye.

"What's the matter Son?"

"Nothing."

"It's obvious that something is wrong with you. Please tell me so I can help you."

"It's Mom. I don't know why, but she seems so different."

"Son, I think I know what it is. Before we got married, your mother was a heavy drinker. She used to drink to numb her pain. Something is bothering her and I have to find out what it is."

"Thank you Dad. I'm so glad you came back. Oh yeah! How is Grandmom?"

"She's doing better. She's being sent home today. She told me not to worry. Although she looked a little weak, she was regaining strength."

"That's great. I was scared that she was going to leave us."

"So was I. We have to make plans to go see her soon."

Jabari and Frankie pulled up into the driveway just as Laurie was returning from the store with her liquor. She stopped in her tracks and stared in horror when she saw Frankie exit the car.

"Frankie!" She said feigning excitement.

"I've been trying to call you. Now I see why you didn't respond. Why didn't you tell me you were coming home?"

"After I saw my mom and she said that she

was okay, I decided to head back home. Where are you coming from?"

"The store."

"What did you buy?"

"What is this, the damn Inquisition?"

"What did you say?" Frankie said shocked that his wife used that language towards him.

"The Inquisition, did you just curse at me?" Frankie was already upset about her drinking; she just overstepped her boundaries.

"Jabari, we'll see you inside," Frankie said as he dismissed Jabari from the conversation.

"Laurie," Frankie said in a loving tone, changing his approach, "Jabari told me that you've been drinking every day since I left. He said you drank until you passed out. What's the matter?"

"I had a dream that you left me for another woman," Laurie said as she collapsed in his arms sobbing.

"So you started drinking over a dream?" Frankie asked wondering if that was all.

"Yes, it seemed so real. It happened while you were in Philadelphia."

"Laurie, I told you before I left and I've told you many times before. I love you and there is no one else for me."

"I know. But those cravings kicked in as soon as you left."

"Why didn't you tell me? We spoke on the phone often; maybe we could have avoided this.

We can kick this problem together like we did before."

"Okay, I'm glad you're back. I feel better already. What happened with Mom?"

"She had a fall and initially they didn't know what the problem was. However, it appears that she lost her balance and fell. She then hit her head and was unconscious when Felicia saw her on floor. But, she's okay and is being discharged today."

"That's great," Laurie said opening her mouth ready to say something else but thought better of it. She really wanted to take that drink.

"I have an idea, let's take that bottle back and get you back on the wagon."

Laurie smiled while biting the inside of her cheek.

"I know it's going to be hard. But the only way to beat this is to meet it head on. Let's go."

Laurie entered the car on the passenger side and agreed to return her liquor. They drove for a while in silence. After ten minutes they were in front of the liquor store. After arriving at the store, Frankie took the bottle and receipt so he could return the liquor.

Meanwhile, Laurie sat in the car waiting for Frankie to return from the liquor store. She looked at him and rolled her eyes. From the look of it, he figured that she really didn't want to return it. But he decided he was going to do whatever it took to help her beat this demon again. He was glad that he decided not to announce his arrival. It looked like she was getting ready for another night of getting drunk and passing out.

"Thank you again," Laurie said as Frankie entered the car.

"You may just have saved my life. Unfortunately, while you were gone, often I would drive to the store while drunk."

"You're talking about me leaving you, it seems like you are the one trying to leave me alone."

"I'm sorry Frankie. I was weak."

Frankie decided to take the long way home. While driving clouds formed, they were dark, heavy laden clouds and there were many air to air lightning strikes. First one big raindrop fell on the car window. Then the barrage of raindrops fell.

The weather is in tune with my feelings today.

"What are you thinking about Laurie?"

"I'm thinking about how much I wanted to drink that liquor."

"I understand. I know that this is going to be difficult for you. We'll take baby steps."

"Frankie, when we get in the house, I want us to go to the room and rest together, okay?"

"No Laurie. I need to see the children and talk to them first."

"No! What the hell?! I thought you were here to support me."

"Laurie, the first time I let you get away with cursing at me. Don't do it again!"

"What the fuck are you going to do about it?"

"What did you say?" He said jerking his head in her direction.

"You heard me, what… the… fuck… are… you… going… to… do… about… it?"

"I know that you are going through withdrawal and this is attributed to your behavior. However, at this time I cannot be around you. Right now I'm ninety-eight hot. You said you want to rest; well, I suggest you take your ass upstairs and calm yourself down. I'll see you later after I talk to our children," he spoke so soft while clenching and unclenching his hands with each word that Laurie barely heard what he said.

Eleven

Laurie headed into the house and straight to her room. Even when she drank in the past, she never spoke to Frankie like that. It's as if someone or something else was inside of her. She went upstairs and prepared to shower. He watched her and wondered what was really going on. After he talked to the children, he was going to see what is bothering his wife.

Laurie set the water as hot as she could handle and went into the shower with so much on her mind. She let the water pour over her head. Using the flowing water from the showerhead to mask her tears, she broke down and cried. She was so angry with herself for cursing and disrespecting Frankie like she did. She didn't know why she did it because Frankie never dishonored her. She just couldn't shake the feeling.

Twenty minutes later Laurie exited the shower. She dried off and applied lotion her entire body while thinking back to the conversation she and Frankie had. The fragrance of vanilla and ginger calmed her. Hoping he joined her, she put on a black satin teddy. Laurie went into their room and fluffed the pillows; while sitting on their bed, she reflected on the day's events. As exhaustion overtook her, she lay down on the pillows and drifted off to sleep.

Bolting straight up in the bed, another bad dream interrupted her sleep. It was so real that it took her five minutes to realize it was a dream. She looked at the clock and realized four hours passed. Lying in the bed beside her was Frankie. A smile formed on her face because she knew for sure she was dreaming.

Her abrupt movement woke Frankie. "Are you okay?"

"I am now," she said kissing him.

"I've been in bed for a while. But you looked like you were enjoying your rest so I refused to wake you up."

"Thank you for being so thoughtful. Frankie, I am sorry about how I spoke with you earlier. I don't know what came over me."

"I think it was a combination of you being tired and having withdrawal from the alcohol. Your apology is accepted. What happened? What made you sit up so quickly?"

"I had that dream again. This time it was more

realistic."

"Tell me about the dream."

"I dreamt that you went to visit your mom because she was sick and she died while you were there. But, while you were there, some woman was interested in you and you were interested in her. You called me and told me that you wanted a divorce."

"Well first of all, we know that Mom is okay now. And as I've told you so many times before, there is no one else for me. I am here for you and you only."

"You're right. I am glad you're home. I really need you."

"I need you too, now get some rest. I want to resume our mini vacation. You need to be well rested," he said winking his eye at her.

I believe him, but I still feel uneasy, she thought to herself.

Twelve

"La hawla la quwatta wa illah billah. What are you talking about Baqir?" Areebah said trying to make sense out of what her son just said.

"I overheard her tell someone on the phone that she injected Abi with the last dosage of morphine and he should be gone within the next thirty minutes."

"What?"

"Sister Areebah…"

"Is what he said true Malika?"

"Ummi, you don't believe me?"

"Baqir, please be quiet for a moment. Malika, please answer me," Areebah said with tears in her eyes.

"I heard the death rattle in his throat. He was on his way out. Your husband has a DNR (do not resuscitate). He also was aware of the protocol of the company."

"And what exactly is that protocol?" Areebah said ready to slap Malika in the face.

"I was instructed when the death rattle sounds, to inject a lethal amount of morphine into him so he can go in peace without pain."

"So, your company believes in mercy killing; euthanasia?"

"I wouldn't say it was a mercy killing. He was about to die, I just helped him transition quicker and without pain."

"Please leave now Malika. I am unable to deal with this now."

"We need to sue Ummi," Baqir said as he calculated how much of the lawsuit money he would receive.

"Baqir, she's right. He is on his last breath. He is in more pain and could not even drink a drop of water from a dropper. It is best that he is allowed to transition smoothly."

Baqir was disappointed. He thought for sure he would receive some money from the lawsuit.

"Areebah, come in here now. Murad is calling for you," Kashifah shouted from the room.

Areebah ran/walked into the room. As she entered, there was an aura of peace in the room.

"Areebah, Baby, come here," Murad said with a whisper as soft as a butterfly's wing.

"Yes Murad, what's going on?"

"Malika is telling you the truth. I did sign a Do Not Resuscitate. I also gave permission for them to inject the final morphine dosage when it appeared that I am close to death. I selected this company because of the way they help people transition from life to death."

Areebah cried as soft as a spring drizzle as Murad told her his decisions.

"But Areebah, the most important thing I want to say is La ilaha il-lAllah, Muhammad dar Rasulullah."

Areebah hugged Murad for a couple of minutes. She stopped hearing his breathing and his body began cooling.

"Inna illahi wa inna ilaihi raji'un (verily from Allah we come and to Him we return)," Areebah said turning to her family.

They all repeated the prayer and left the room.

Tears flowed from all of their eyes. Their emotions were mixed. They went from sad that he passed to relief knowing that it was better for him to leave the pain. They were also pleased that he recited the kalimah Shahadah - profession of faith - prior to him moving to the next stage.

Malika knew it wasn't long before Murad would pass so she didn't leave as instructed by Areebah.

"Sister Areebah, your husband already picked out a funeral director and the masjid where he wants his janazah (funeral prayer) to be performed. Would you like me to call?"

"Yes Malika, please do. And thank you for not leaving when I told you."

"You're welcome."

After thirty minutes the funeral director arrived and pronounced Murad dead. He then prepared the death certificate. Meanwhile, Areebah was in the other room calling, texting, and messaging people about Murad's death. She encouraged everyone to spread the word.

"Ummi, did Abi have life insurance?"

"Why do you ask Baqir?"

"I just wanted to know. How are we paying for the funeral," he said lying to his mother.

Baqir knew that his parents were always prepared for their death because he remembered them often telling him to live in this world as if you will live forever or die today. He'd been having financial problems and any health insurance his dad would have for him would be helpful. However, Baqir didn't want to look greedy and coldhearted.

"I just know that paying for a janazah can be expensive and I wondered if you have enough to pay for it."

"Baqir, you know that we knew about your father's death for a while now. He wouldn't leave us without the necessary paperwork and funds."

"Oh, okay Ummi."

Baqir decided that it was too early to ask his mom about any funds that he will receive because according to the Qur'an, he should receive a portion equal to two shares of the daughter. He decided he would wait a few days before bringing the subject up again.

"Baqir, I want to talk to you!" Sahlah said grabbing him into the kitchen.

"Everyone knows you need money. But damn, couldn't you wait until the body was cold? Let Ummi deal with her grief, while we lost a father, Ummi lost her soul mate. She may spend the rest of her life alone."

Thirteen

"I can never get tired of seeing this place," Laurie said as she and Frankie walked into the posh hotel where they started their getaway before he had to go to Philadelphia to see about his mother.

"It is breathtaking isn't it? The sights you see pale in comparison to you. You take my breath away and I am so happy and grateful that you are my wife."

Laurie rushed into Frankie's arms and their lips locked. All the negative thoughts and horrible nightmares vanished in their embrace. At that moment, it was just Frankie and Laurie. He had to pull himself away from her so he could go check in and retrieve their room keys.

Laurie didn't think it was possible. However, she loved Frankie more today than she ever did. She couldn't wait to get into the room. This time she insisted on him joining her in the heart-shaped whirlpool. The last time he surprised her, but this time she had some surprises of her own.

"Alright Baby, I have the keys. This time we're in room 1102. I bet you the view from there is magnificent."

Laurie couldn't wait to get up to the eleventh floor. Although she enjoyed the first room they had, there was no spectacular view. As the elevator ascended and reached the eleventh floor, Laurie was gushing with love for her husband. She could not wait for them to get into the room and slip into something more comfortable.

"Enter into our love palace," Frankie said ushering Laurie into the room.

The room was decorated with burgundy and black satin sheets and comforters. The carpet was black with burgundy concentric circles. The drapery matched the carpet. On the bed were rose petals and chocolate covered strawberries. When they entered the room, there were cinnamon and vanilla candles lit with the hot tub filled with a tropical fragranced bubble bath.

"Frankie, I thought you had to check in? How did you get the room with my favorite scents?"

"Ancient Chinese secret," he said in jest.

"Ancient Chinese secret, huh?" Laurie said playing along.

They walked over to the window to see the view.

"You've got to be kidding me," Frankie said

losing his cool demeanor.

"What?"

"The only view in this room is over the dining area."

"Are you serious? I thought you came here earlier?"

"I did. But I was working on getting everything right in the room that I didn't look out the window."

"Well, the view I want is right here," she said sashaying towards him.

"And the view I want is walking right towards me."

"Let's bathe together," Laurie said.

"But you love bathing. I want you to enjoy yourself."

"I'll enjoy myself sooo much better with you in the water with me."

They disrobed and headed into the bathroom.

"This water feels good," Laurie said.

"Yeah," Frankie said as he grimaced, feeling his skin melt away.

Ring. Ring. Ring.

"Not the phone again, I don't know if I can take another cancellation," Laurie said.

"I'm not going to let anything ruin our time. I'm not answering."

Ring. Ring. Ring.

"Answer the phone," Laurie said preparing for the worst.

"HELLO!"

"Frankie, I know you and Laurie are out. But, I need to talk to you, it's important."

"What's so important that you can't wait until the weekend is over Mom?"

"Do you remember Areebah?"

"Yeah, what about her?"

"Well, her husband just died."

"And why are you telling me this? I'm in here with my wife and you're calling me for this. Mom, I'll call you later. Right now I need to be with my wife."

Laurie was proud at the way Frankie stood up to his mom. But, what was she talking about. No, better yet, who was she talking about. Laurie decided not to let it bother her and to spend her time loving her husband.

After they spent time together in the tub, Laurie put on her satin slip and Frankie put on his lounge pants and t-shirt and they ordered room service. While waiting, Laurie dozed off to sleep.

Frankie, do you remember her from a long time ago? I want you to meet her. I know that you and Laurie are happy, but I always wanted you to marry her.

Laurie bolted up out of her sleep.

"What's the matter Baby?" Frankie said concerned because Laurie's face was flush and she looked like she saw a ghost.

"Frankie, I had that dream again. This time it was your mom telling you about this woman and how she always wanted you to marry her."

"Come here Baby."

Frankie wiped Laurie's eyes and hugged her tight. She shivered with fear.

What are these dreams telling me? She said to herself while Frankie held and consoled her.

"It will be okay Areebah."

"Areebah! Who the fuck is Areebah?"

Frankie looked up confused. He couldn't believe that he just called Laurie Areebah. How can he calm her down?

"I'm sorry baby. I just received a call from my mom that an old friend of mine husband just passed. I don't know why I said her name."

"Maybe because you've been thinking about her since you left Philly."

"What?!"

"I told you I kept having dreams about a woman and all of a sudden you're holding me and calling another woman's name."

"As I told you before Laurie, I want no one but you. I haven't seen Areebah in thirty-five years. I didn't even think about her until my mom just called and told me about her husband."

"Why would your mom call and tell you that?"

"Well, that's what my mom does. She always tells me about people that were in my life before you."

"What are you insinuating?"

"Look Laurie, let's not argue. I brought you here so we could love one another. I'm a lover not a fighter," Frankie said turning on the charm.

"Well, there won't be any loving tonight. I'm going downstairs to get a drink."

"I thought you were on the wagon and no longer drinking."

"Well, after my husband calls me another woman's name as we are having a romantic evening, what would you suggest I do? Just sit around and watch you reminisce about another woman?"

"Okay, then go. There's nothing I can say to convince you otherwise and I don't feel like arguing anymore. I'll be here waiting for you."

Laurie stamped out the room and slammed the door with extra emphasis. Frankie sat in the burgundy oversized hotel chair. He closed his eyes. First he thought about Laurie and her angry outbursts. Then his thoughts drifted off to why his mother would disturb him during this special time with his wife. Then, his thoughts drifted to Areebah. He wondered how she was doing.

While Laurie was gone, Frankie decided to go on social media. As he logged on, he checked to see if Areebah accepted his friend request. When he was in Philly earlier and his mother mentioned her to him he requested her as a friend on the website. But, after he arrived home, he never checked the site again. But he saw that not only did she accept his friend request, she sent him a private message. He responded but didn't want to get too involved because he knew Laurie would return soon. After responding, he logged off.

He then decided to call his mother for additional information.

"Hey Mom.

"Hey Son, what's up? I thought you and Laurie were having a romantic getaway?"

"There's that special word, were. After you called, I was hugging Laurie and I guess my mind drifted to Areebah. I mistakenly called out Areebah's name."

"You did what?!"

"Well Mom, what were you thinking calling me with that information? I'm sure it could have waited."

"You're right son. My timing was horrible. However, I just wanted you to know."

"Well now that I do, did you happen to get her number?"

Laurie walked in the room and saw Frankie on the phone. She overheard his conversation and couldn't believe her ears.

"Get whose number?" She said.

Fourteen

Areebah overheard her children speaking. They were not aware that she and Murad discussed in excess what she should do with her life after he died. He encouraged her to remarry. And after her mother told her about Frankie, she could think of nothing else.

"My beloved children," she said, "don't worry about me.

Your dad and I discussed so many things in this two month period. As for you Mr. Baqir, I know that you are in financial straits, but can't you wait at least until we give your father his rights and bury him before discussing any money you may receive?"

Baqir felt ashamed because he didn't want to appear insensitive. But since he had to come and be down here with his family, he lost his job. His boss told him if he left he'd better not come back. This was his father dying. What was he supposed to do? Not spend the last few days with his father? Baqir decided his father was more important.

What he didn't count on was his girlfriend telling him that she was pregnant. First of all they're not married and his mother would not accept the relationship. Next, she knew they were struggling, why wasn't birth control or contraceptive used? Baqir began crying because it seemed like his entire world was crashing upon him. Instead of taking his complaints to the creation, Baqir decided to give it all to the Creator.

Baqir went into the salah (prayer) room and prepared himself to perform a few Sunnah (not obligatory) prayers to calm him down. His future depended on the inheritance. He already calculated it and he should get at least $750,000.00 not including any life insurance.

Fifteen

After the visitors stopped visiting, Areebah started going through Murad's belongings. One day she was feeling lonely and she decided to go on a social networking site to see if Frankie replied to her private message. After she logged in, she saw a notification for a private message. To her chagrin, it was a response from Frankie.

"Hello to you," read his response.

"☺" She responded.

She left the computer open and continued cleaning the house. She wasn't sure how often he used social networking because prior to responding to her private message, his last post was more than two years ago. However, she left it open just in case he decided to reply.

Since Murad died, Areebah involved herself more with the Islamic community. She met many nice sisters. There's one sister with whom she clicked. She decided to call her because she needed someone to talk to.

"As salaamu alaikum, Ra'ifah."

"Wa laikum mus salaam Areebah, how have you been?"

"Alhamdulillah, I feel like I'm getting better every day."

"I remember you telling me that Murad encouraged you to get remarried. Your iddah (waiting period of four months ten days) period is up. Have you decided to get remarried yet?"

"Not quite," Areebah said not wanting to share with her friend her interest in Frankie.

"Well, from what I understand, there are a lot of brothers interested in you. Are you interested in being married in polygyny?"

"Nah, not at this time. I think I'll give myself a little more time, in shaa Allah."

"In shaa Allah."

While talking to Ra'ifah, Areebah heard a notification from the social networking page. She needed to get Ra'ifah off the phone in case it was Frankie responding.

"Well Ra'ifah, I have to get going. I'll call you either later today or tomorrow, in shaa Allah."

"Okay Areebah, make sure you take good care of yourself. Know that I love you fisabillillah (for the sake of Allah)."

"As do I, as salaamu alaikum."

"Wa laikum mus salaam."

Areebah rushed to the computer to see what the notification was.

"Hello Areebah," Frankie responded.

He responded! What do I say now?

"How are you? It's been a long time. My mother told me you were asking about me. How's life?" She responded.

"Life is life. How's life with you?"

"It's good, Alhamdulillah. I mean all praises due to Allah."

"I see you are still practicing Islam. That's great. Well, I have to go now. I just wanted to let you know that you can chat with me anytime you want."

"Okay, take care."

What does that mean? Is he not as happily married as my mother told me?

Areebah decided to take a break from going through Murad's items. She decided to call her mother.

"As salaamu alaikum Ummi."

"Wa laikum mus salaam Areebah. How have you been? I haven't heard from you in a while."

"I'm well. I am more active in the community now so I stay busy. Also, I decided to work on my business full time. It's good to have something to do so I can stay busy."

"That's good. So what do I owe this call from my only child?"

"Now that I've completed my iddah, I'm thinking of moving back to Philadelphia. I've spent this time to clear my mind and although I've become active in the community, I don't feel this is my home anymore. My children aren't here and my beloved Murad is gone; I need a sense of family."

"I understand Habibti (My love), when are you planning on moving?"

"In about two weeks."

"Okay, we'll get your room together."

"That sounds good. Also, I decided to see if I could get in contact with Frankie and he responded to my message on the internet. He told me I can message him anytime I'd like. Are you sure he's happily married?"

"The last time I talked to Inez he was."

"Okay, we'll see. How's Abi?"

"He's doing okay."

Ding. Areebah heard another notification from the internet. She was surprised that Frankie would contact her again so soon.

"I have to go Ummi. I have something to do. As salaamu alaikum."

"Wa laikum salaam Baby. Take care of yourself."

"I will."

Areebah rushed to the computer to read the notification.

"I don't know who you are, but you need to stop chatting with my husband. I don't care whether he told you that you can chat with him anytime or not."

Sixteen

"I have to go Mom. I'll talk to you later."

"Alright Son, be smart and be careful."

"I will. I love you."

"I love you too, later."

Frankie disconnected the phone and turned to face Laurie. The disdain in her face spoke volumes along with the strong stench of alcohol let Frankie know that what was to come was a ferocious conversation that would not end well. He decided to not let the conversation get too far out of hand.

"Whose phone number were you asking your mother for?" Laurie said forcing Frankie to admit to asking for Areebah's number.

"What are you doing back here? I thought you were going to drink?" He said raising his voice trying to deflect her anger.

"Don't worry about me and my drinking.

Answer my question."

"Fine, I was asking for Areebah's number."

"Even after you know how much it upsets me?" Laurie said trying to stable herself.

"Well you went drinking even though you know how much it upsets me."

"Our romantic excursion is officially over. I'm ready to go!"

"I'm not going anywhere Laurie. This room is already paid for and I am not able to get another refund. How about we both forget about the past hour and make the best of this?"

"I'll try. But I hope your mother doesn't call again."

The rest of the weekend went well and they were in a good place again. Frankie didn't know that while he rested Laurie went through his phone and saw his message to Areebah. She left a response to make sure Areebah knew not to contact her husband again.

"Thank you for demanding that we stay. I truly enjoyed myself," Laurie said to Frankie as they headed back home.

"I did too. I love you Laurie. I'm so sorry for the pain I caused you."

"Apology accepted. Just know that I do love you and I cannot imagine not being with you as your friend and wife. I'll do anything to keep us together. Remember that."

They rode the rest of the way in silence.

Seventeen

"Hey Babe," Frankie said to Laurie while tapping her butt and kissing her.

"How are you today?" He said.

"I'm having a fantastic day. Have I told you how much I love you today?"

"Nope, do tell," he said never turning down an opportunity for her to tell him that she loved him.

"Well, the kids are in school…" she said. She could never get enough of her husband.

"Alright Baby," he said smiling.

Although they had trying times these past few months, they decided that there were always ups and downs in marriages. They wanted to make sure that their highs were better than their worse lows. The worst of it was when Laurie intercepted a message from Areebah. It took three weeks before she spoke to Frankie.

"Meet me in the room," Laurie said with a raspy voice.

"I'm on my way!"

Ring. Ring. Ring.

Not again! Frankie thought.

"Are you going to get the phone Baby?"

"Nope, this is our time," Frankie said muting the phone.

They embraced each other and tasted each other as their lips and tongues locked. They moved towards the bed. Frankie pulled the brown and black sateen comforter and tan satin sheet down and fluffed the pillows to make sure his wife was comfortable. Laurie slipped out of her champagne satin slip. Frankie unbuttoned and unzipped his pants.

Buzz. Buzz. Buzz.

"You've got to be kidding me!" Frankie said.

"Answer it Frankie, it must be important."

"Hello!" Frankie said yelling into the phone.

"Hello Frankie," Felicia said.

Frankie hasn't heard from his sister since he left Philly six months ago. Why was she calling him now he wondered? His annoyance changed to concern.

"Mom's in the hospital," Felicia said with a lump in her throat. "I really didn't want to call you but this time it's critical. The doctor said she has less than a month to live."

"What?!" He said louder than intended.

"What's the matter with her? When I spoke

with her a couple of weeks ago, she told me she was okay."

"I called her earlier this morning and she did not answer so I rushed to her house. When I arrived, she was on the floor. She was nonresponsive so I called the ambulance and rushed her to the hospital. They were able to get her to respond. However, when she arrived at the hospital they took her to get some tests. It showed that she had several mini strokes. She's been having them since her first fall but no one caught it."

"I thought she was going to the doctor for follow up."

"She did and they asked her how she felt and she always said everything was okay."

"Didn't they factor in her earlier fall?"

"I guess she didn't show any signs of trauma so they took her at her word. Anyway, while at the hospital, they said the mini strokes caused irreparable damage and that they don't expect her to live more than thirty days."

"I'll be on the next plane to Philadelphia. Which hospital is she in?"

"She's at the same hospital as last time."

"I'll pick you up from the airport when you arrive."

"Don't worry about that, I'll rent a car. I'd rather have transportation so I don't have to depend on anyone."

As Frankie disconnected the call, Laurie

became worried. She didn't want Frankie going to Philly without her. She hugged him tight for a long time and let him cry and grieve his mother's illness.

"I'm going with you," she said.

"No, the children are in school and at this time I don't know that status of my mother's health. When I arrive at the hospital, I will call you with an updated status and then we can determine when you and the children need to come up."

"Okay," she said planning on purchasing plane tickets as soon as he leaves.

While Frankie was making the necessary travel arrangements, Laurie suppressed her anger and began packing his bags; making sure that he did not leave anything behind. After they were done, she told him, "It's cold in Philly now so I packed extra socks and sweaters for you. Also, all of your cosmetics are in this compartment. I also packed you sneakers and dress shoes. Is there anything else you need me to pack for you?"

"No Baby. I love you so much and I appreciate you taking your time to pack my luggage for me. I am going to miss you and I'm sorry that we couldn't finish what we started. And remember; don't worry about Areebah or anyone else. I'm going for my mom and we will be back together very soon."

"That's the least of your worries now. Go and see what's happening with your mom. I'll be here waiting for you and preparing to make love to you in ways that you can't imagine."

Upon hearing that, Frankie had a smile on his face and was on his way to the airport. I really love my wife. I wish she wouldn't worry about me leaving her. I cannot imagine a life without her and thank God for putting her in my life and making her my wife.

After a while, Frankie boarded the airplane and was fast asleep. He did not realize how tired he was until it was time for them to land at PHL (Philadelphia International Airport). Frankie did not recollect any of the announcements from the flight attendants. He disembarked from the plane and went downstairs to baggage claim. After waiting for fifteen minutes for his luggage, they finally came out. He then headed over to the buses and boarded the bus for the rental car agency.

After renting his car, Frankie headed straight to the hospital. He did not know what to expect but he expected the worst and hoped for the best. As he was giving the valet the keys to the car, Frankie bumped into his sister.

Eighteen

Kashifah went to visit Inez in the hospital. As soon as she entered the room, the two embraced.

"It's been a month of Sundays since I've last seen you Inez."

"Girl, I know. I always said I was going to call you but life got in the way."

"I was so shocked when I heard you were in the hospital. How are you feeling?"

"Honestly, not too hot. I don't think I'll be around by the year's end."

"Well, I'll make du'a for you."

"Thanks Kashifah."

"Did I tell you that Areebah moved back to Philly?"

Inez and Kashifah were friends since the late 60s and early 70s. Inez's husband was arrested in the early 70s and sentenced to real life. Kashifah was an officer with the Black Panther Party. Both of them encouraged the improvement of knowledge and self-determination within the Black community. After her husband was imprisoned, Inez was a single mom for many years prior to getting remarried. Kashifah and her husband, Shafaat, remained married and accepted Al-Islam as their way of life.

Shafaat and Inez always bumped heads so after a while, Kashifah and Inez lost contact. Both mothers thought their children would get married but when they left the city for college in two different regions of the country, it seemed as if that was not going to be. Then, when Frankie moved to San Diego and married Laurie, it became obvious that the two of them will never be married.

"No!" Inez said perking up.

"Well," Kashifah said, "Areebah's husband passed away a year ago. She was down in Dallas alone because both of her children no longer lived with her nor were they living in Dallas. So, Shafaat and I encouraged her to move back home and be near us. She took us up on our offer."

"That's great!" Inez said.

"Frankie is on his way to see me. Maybe we can plan for them to meet each other. He's coming without his wife."

"I'll set it up," Kashifah said, "but, I cannot let Shafaat know. He never wanted them to be together because Frankie is not Muslim."

"Well, it's not like they can be together," Inez said with trepidation, "Frankie is still married to Laurie and they have a wonderful marriage. I just think it would be nice for the two of them to see each other while he is here. Do me a favor. Have Areebah stop by to see me as soon as possible so I can help her set up the meeting."

"Okay," Kashifah said smiling inside and out. When they were younger, they wanted Frankie and Areebah to be together and it made her heart feel good that they will see each other again after thirty-five years.

"Inez, on another note, I have something serious to ask you."

"What's that Kashifah?"

"Have you ever considered taking your Shahadah (declaration of faith)?"

"I have at times. Why do you ask?"

"You are close to death and I love you. I would feel guilty if I didn't do my job and invite you to Al-Islam."

"But it's too late for me."

"Inez. It's never too late until you no longer are breathing."

"I have considered it. Since leaving the Party, I've delved into different religions and denominations but I never learned about Islam. None of the other religions interested me. What is it that I must do to become Muslim?"

"First, do you believe that there is one God

and he has no partners or children?"

"Yes, that has always been one of my problems with many of the religions. I couldn't understand how there could be more than one God. So, yes, that is a belief I've always had."

"Second, do you believe that Muhammad, from more than 1434 years ago is the last prophet and messenger of Allah?"

"I did read up on him and based on my readings, I cannot see how he is not a prophet and messenger."

"Well, My friend, with these beliefs you are a Muslim. It only takes the belief in the oneness of Allah and that Prophet Muhammad is the last prophet and messenger."

"At this time I will say that I have both of those beliefs and I will embrace Al-Islam."

"I'll have to come back later and have some witnesses so that it is known that you decided to embrace Islam. As a matter of fact, when you see Areebah, you can let her know about this and then we can make arrangements."

"Thank you Kashifah," Inez said as her eyes began to water. "I am glad that you took the time to share this with me."

"You're welcome Inez. I'm going to leave you now so I can get in contact with Areebah. I love you and I pray for ease for you in this world and the next."

"I love you too," Inez said believing this was the last time she'll see her friend.

As soon as Kashifah left the hospital she called Areebah and told her that it was urgent that she meet her. Areebah was concerned because the last time she received a call similar to that, she was getting the information saying that her husband was gravely ill. She met with her mother within ten minutes.

"As salaamu alaikum," Kashifah said.

"Wa laikum mus salaam Ummi. What's the matter? Are you sick?"

"No, I am not sick. However, remember when I was talking to you about Inez, Frankie's mom a while ago?"

"Of course I do," Areebah said.

"Well, she is in the hospital. She is very ill and is not expected to last until the end of the year. Frankie is coming to town today and Inez and I thought the two of you should meet."

Since Areebah and Frankie's been communicating for a while, she knew his mother was sick. She also knew that he was coming to town. However, neither of them let anyone know that they communicated. Areebah feigned surprise. However, she wondered where her mother was going with all of this information. It shocked her to hear that her mother and Frankie's mom wanted them to meet.

"Well," Kashifah said with the excitement of a school girl, "Inez and I think you should make a chance meeting with Frankie. He is happily married; however, after his mother passes, he may not come back to Philly. So, this chance meeting will give you two the opportunity to sit down and reminisce about the past and talk about what could have been."

"Wow Ummi!" Areebah said. "I thought you and Abi didn't want me to be anywhere near Frankie because he is a kafir (disbeliever)."

"I'm glad you brought that up," Kashifah said with caution, "don't mention this conversation to your father."

Areebah looked at her mother as if she is seeing her for the first time. She never thought her mother kept any secrets from her father. As a matter of fact, her name means revealer of secrets and she is the total opposite. This does sound like a good idea. I've been having lunch and dinner with many of the brothers here and many of them aren't about anything. They either say they want a Khadijah (an older woman who is financially well off) or they want to be overbearing.

"Areebah," her mother said startling her from her thoughts, "I'm serious; do not tell your father anything."

"Okay, I won't," she said. "When does Frankie arrive and where will he be?"

"I don't have all of the particulars. However, Inez asked me to have you come visit her as soon as you can at the hospital. Oh yeah, I forgot to mention that she wants to embrace Al-Islam. She and I had a long talk and this is what she wants. It needs to be done so she can die as a believer"

"SubhanAllah, that's great!" Areebah said thinking to herself that if Inez is interested in Islam, Frankie may not be that far away from accepting Islam.

"What hospital and what is her room number? Also, what is her last name in case they ask me that at the security desk?"

"She's at the University Hospital downtown in room 712. Her name is Inez Williams."

"Okay Ummi, I'm going right now."

"Love you Baby."

"I love you too Ummi."

Instead of driving to the hospital Areebah decided to take public transportation because it was quicker and less expensive to catch the El and walk over to Chestnut Street rather than fight through traffic and then pay exorbitant prices for parking downtown. She was surprised that she had butterflies. Although she befriended Ra'ifah, she didn't deem her a close friend and since she is the only child, she had to keep this rendezvous between herself, her mother, and Inez.

Areebah arrived at the hospital within thirty minutes of speaking with her mother and was at the security desk waiting for a visitor's pass. As she was getting closer to seeing Inez and in time Frankie, she was getting more excited. She entered the elevator and her thoughts roamed to seeing Frankie in the flesh after all these years.

Areebah exited the elevator on the seventh

floor and many emotions rushed to her. She remembered being in the hospital when Murad was sick; she started feeling lightheaded. Sadness crept over her. Before she knew it, she was in front of Inez's door. She was just about to chicken out and go back on the elevator when Frankie's sister Felicia opened the door.

"Areebah!" She said in glee. "Mom told me you were coming to see her. How have you been? Sorry to hear about your husband?"

Felicia hugged Areebah like she was a long lost friend. The last time Areebah saw her she was eight years of age. Time sure flies. Areebah had to stifle her fears and walk into the room with Inez.

"Ms. Inez," Areebah said with tears in her eyes at seeing her lying in the hospital bed.

"Don't be sad Areebah," Inez said trying to console her.

"I wanted you to come here under happy situations, not sad ones."

"I know it has to be difficult for you to be here. Your mom told me about your husband. Sorry for your loss."

"Thank you Ms. Inez," Areebah said trying to put on that façade she is famous for.

"Did your mom tell you that Frankie will be coming to town?"

"Yes she did."

"Well, he is set to be here in a few minutes. Go to the end of the hall in the waiting room area and read a magazine or whatever reading material they have. He phoned us from the airport and said he had his luggage and rental car. Therefore, he should be here any minute. I am going to send his sister to the lobby and she's going to act like she couldn't stand being here with me any longer. They will walk in together that way you will know who he is."

Now Areebah understood why Frankie's sister hugged her so tight. It seemed as if the entire family was in on this "chance" meeting. She was all for it though. Ever since speaking with her mother an hour ago, all she could think about was Frankie.

"Areebah," Inez said snapping her out of her daydreaming, "you need to get moving now, Frankie just called and said he is giving his keys to the valet."

Areebah rushed to the waiting room and did all she could to contain herself. When she saw Frankie and his sister exit the elevator, she almost jumped into his arms. Although he looked sad, she could just imagine the smile on his face. The plan Inez came up with was that after a few minutes she would tell Frankie that she's tired and she wants to rest for a few minutes. His sister will suggest that he go to the café across the street from the hospital. As he headed out, Areebah would take the next elevator downstairs and be a few hundred feet behind him and will enter the café after him and make sure she was not in his line of vision.

"Hey Sis," he said hugging her for dear life.

"Where are you going?"

"I can't be in that room any longer. I held vigil as long as I could and I knew that you should be arriving soon."

"I'm glad that we ran into each other," she said with tears in her eyes.

"Mom is not doing too well. Let me walk you to her room so you can hug and talk to her. She's been asking for you."

"Okay," he said wondering what was in store for him.

Frankie and Felicia headed to their mother's room. When he arrived, she was lying there looking peaceful. He did not want to awaken her; but, as he turned to leave the room she opened her eyes and gave him a wide smile. He was happy to see his mother smile; however, he could see that she's lost a lot of weight and her strength was a fraction of what it was when he last saw her.

"So Mom," he said.

"How long have you known that you were sick?"

"Aww Baby," she said unable to speak pass a whisper, "the doctor just gave us the prognosis."

"That's not what I'm asking," he said with much sadness and hurt in his voice.

"Every day I talk to you and ask you how you're doing, your response is always, 'I'm doing well.' But look, obviously you weren't."

"Don't be mad at me Frankie," Inez said, "I didn't want to worry you all."

"When I came here six months ago you said there was nothing wrong with you. However, you had to have some symptoms."

"All of you have your lives to live and I'm an old woman anyway."

"It doesn't matter if you're an old woman. We love you and we'd rather you would have told us than kept it a secret."

"I understand that. But you all don't have to worry about anything; I've taken care of everything for my impending death."

Frankie couldn't believe his ears. His mother was talking in a businesslike manner as usual.

"Mom," he said, "I just arrived and I need to get some coffee. I noticed a café across the street and I am going there to purchase some coffee. I'll be back shortly."

Frankie headed to the café with a lot on his mind. He wondered how much more time his mother had.

"Laurie, Mom's not doing well. Purchase the air tickets for you and the children. You all need to get here as soon as you can," Frankie left the message on Laurie's phone. He hoped she wasn't so depressed that she started drinking again.

Frankie entered the café with a lot on his mind and stood in line to place his order. He was not aware that someone was following him and standing three people behind him in line.

Everything was going well because Frankie was so preoccupied about his mother and talking on the phone to someone that he wasn't paying attention to his surroundings. After Frankie placed his order, he turned around to view his surroundings. For a brief moment, he and Areebah locked eyes.

He thought he saw Areebah so he looked more intent at the woman. However, he knew that Muslim women didn't like being accosted so he brushed it off as wishful thinking. She moved a little behind the person in front of her and began fidgeting with her phone acting like she had a text or was reading something on her phone. Frankie decided that he was seeing things and went back to the counter waiting for his order.

Areebah placed her order and kept looking at Frankie without him seeing her. She just finished placing her order when the cashier called his name. She picked up her coffee and paid the cashier. The cashier was taking a long time giving her the change that she told her to keep it as a tip. When Frankie turned around to pick up his order, Areebah walked towards him at a slow pace with her head down so that when he turned around her he would bump into her.

"Excuse me," Frankie said after bumping into the woman.

"No, excuse me," Areebah said with a voice reminiscence of Dorothy Dandridge.

This caused Frankie to look up and to his surprise stood the first woman he ever loved. Looking in her big, almond shaped brown eyes, Frankie smiled the biggest smile since he heard of his mother's illness.

"Areebah!" He said. "I knew that was you."

"Frankie!"

"Why didn't you tell me you planned on meeting me when I came to town?" he said.

"I wanted to surprise you. It was great chatting with you on the web; however, I felt it would be even better to see you in person. Also, your mom and my mom wanted us to meet up so I played along with their plan."

"Well, it's a great plan. I need this relief. I don't know who else I can talk to about my mother's illness. I am sure that she won't be with us for much longer."

"Have you seen her yet?" She said knowing that he just left the room.

"She's resting right now."

"Okay, well, let's sit over there so we can talk."

"Sounds good; you look much better than your photos. I am so glad that you are here."

"Thank you," He said as his cheeks reddened.

"Did your family come with you?"

"No, we didn't know the extent of my mother's illness. I just called my wife and told her to purchase air tickets so she and the children can see my mom. So we have at least a day to hang out."

"That's great," She said still remembering the message Laurie wrote to her from his account.

"How are your parents?" He said.

"They're doing well."

For a few moments Frankie and Areebah sat in an uncomfortable silence. Each had a barrage of questions and statements they wanted to say to the other but didn't know how to start. Areebah then thought about the one thing that linked them.

"Frankie," she said loving the way his name sounded when she spoke it.

"Yes."

"Do you remember when we used to march to the cadences?"

"I sure do," he said perking up.

"I don't know what it's been said," he said.

"Richard Nixon is a pig," she said.

They both started laughing. Many people don't understand but the children of the struggle, that is the children of the members of the Black Panther Party had a different upbringing than most people in the United States. In addition to singing cadences, they also participated in social boycotts. They were also taught that there are always rats in every organization so trusting people is difficult; that is, everyone has the propensity of being an infiltrator. The most important lesson was that there were certain people whose name you just didn't say. Because of that she did not ask him about his father. They sat for a little longer and reminisced about their past. Then Frankie received a call that disturbed him.

"I have to get back to the hospital," he said looking in her eyes as tears began to form.

"I understand."

"Here's my number if you ever need a shoulder to cry on."

She knew Frankie was married, but she was tired of being the "good" girl. She saw something she wanted and she was going after it. She concluded that she had a day or so to share with him before his wife showed up and she was going to benefit as much as she could because she knew after he returned, they will only be able to communicate via the web, maybe.

Nineteen

Frankie headed toward the hospital and Areebah headed toward the El. She then decided that she was going to show him what type of support she could offer so she walked back to the hospital. After getting another visitor's pass, Areebah entered the elevator and went to the seventh floor; her stomach was turning somersaults knowing that she would be able to be there for Frankie, even if just for a day. When she turned the corner, it was as if someone kicked her in the belly.

As she exited the elevator and turned the corner, she saw Frankie embracing a beautiful woman. She knew that woman had to be Laurie. Shocked to see her, Areebah froze in place. At the same time, Laurie looked over and saw her standing there.

Laurie whispered something in Frankie's ear

and he snapped his head around. For a fraction of a second he smiled and then the weight of the situation showed on his face. Laurie's body tensed and Frankie rushed her into his mother's room.

"What is she doing here?" Laurie said in a hushed tone.

"I guess my sister called and told her that my mom took a turn for the worse," Frankie lied.

"I thought you were here to see your mom. Why does she look like she saw a ghost when she saw me?"

"Are you asking me to read someone else's mind? This is neither the time nor place. We will discuss it later."

Felicia, recognizing and feeling the tension performed the performance of her life.

"Areebah! Thank you for coming. It's been a long time since we've seen you Mom's not doing too well."

Family was something, Areebah thought; they would protect their family members no matter how long the family member had been married.

"Felicia thanks for calling me," she hugged Felicia.

"Thank you for stepping in; I didn't know what to do," she whispered in Felicia's ear.

"Although I like Laurie, I always wanted you to marry Frankie. Never tell anyone I said that," Felicia whispered back.

"How's Ms. Inez?" Areebah said showing that

she had familiarity with the family.

"She's not doing too well," Frankie said too soon.

"I'm sorry to hear that. I just came to check up on her. I'm leaving so you all can have family time with your mother. I know how it is to lose a loved one. I recently lost my husband and it was difficult on me and my children."

"Aren't you going to introduce me to your friend Felicia," Laurie said trying to sound sweet, but the bitterness was evident.

"Excuse my rudeness. Areebah this is Laurie, Frankie's wife. Laurie, Areebah, an old family friend."

"You look so familiar," Laurie said letting Areebah know that she was aware of who she was, "didn't I see you on Frankie's friends list on the web?"

"It's possible," Areebah said.

"I have thousands of friends from the past. It was a pleasure meeting you," Areebah lied.

"And you," Laurie lied as well.

"Well, it was good seeing all of you again. I have to go."

Areebah hurried into the elevator and was thankful when the doors closed.

"Astaghfirullah (Allah forgive me)!" She said just loud enough for her to hear. "I can't believe I behaved like that. 'Audhu billahi minash shaitan nir rajeem (I seek refuge with Allah from the accursed Shaitan (devil)). I really thought I had a couple of days with him. Why is his wife here already?"

Inez perished a couple of days later. Because Inez knew she was dying, she requested her children to have her funeral the day after she passed. The day after the funeral Inez set an appointment with her attorney for the will reading. Once all of this was completed, Frankie and his family headed back home. Areebah and Frankie saw each other for a fleeting second at the funeral but neither said a word to the other. The last time they spoke was at the café before Laurie arrived.

Frankie and Laurie rode to the airport in silence as well as on the flight back to San Diego. The children observed their parents' silence and were concerned. The last time the children observed their parents being this distant from each other was when their mom was drinking. Jabari remembered hearing the name Areebah and then seeing a Muslim woman stealing looks at his father when she thought no one was looking. Is this what was causing the tension between his mom and dad? For the moment, Jabari just remained the cautious observer.

When they arrived home, Frankie and the boys took the luggage in the house and Laurie began washing the dirty laundry from the long trip. She decided that now was the time and place to have the "Areebah" talk.

"Frankie, Honey," she said mustering up as

much sweetness as she can despite the situation.

"Yeah Babe," he said knowing what to expect. Ever since Areebah walked around that hospital corner, Laurie's been silent. Laurie's silence meant she was calculating something and coming to her conclusions.

"We need to talk," she said with all honesty.

"I know."

"After that incident with you and Areebah messaging each other on the web you told me you wouldn't contact her anymore. Why was she at the hospital?"

"Felicia told you that she called her to come and see Mom," Frankie said sticking with the script.

"And only a blind man would believe that lie," Laurie said screeching.

"What do you mean by that?"

"When she turned that corner and saw me, she was like a deer in the headlights. It was as if she knew you were in town but thought I was not. Why would she behave like that?"

"Again, you want me to be a mind reader. Just ask me what you want to ask?"

"Did you two sleep together?"

"No, not at all," he said with all honesty. Not mentioning that when he saw her in the café he was wondering how it would be to be with her. But he dare not say that to his wife.

"Then why did she look so dejected when she saw me hugging you – MY husband – in the hospital?"

"Are you asking me to read someone else's mind? Really?"

"I'm not asking you to read someone else's mind; but, I can tell something is there. You avoided her at all costs. I think you made sure our paths didn't cross."

"Then she had the audacity to make it a point to let me know that her husband is deceased. Who does that?"

"What are you talking about? She was just sympathizing with us."

"Whatever!"

"I love you Laurie. I love being married to you and there is no one else in the world I would rather be with than you," Frankie meant most of the words he was saying; although he was still thinking about Areebah.

Did she really say the thing about her husband to stake a claim to me? He wondered fascinated with how forward she's become. She used to always be the "good and shy" girl.

"There is definitely something you're not telling me."

"I spoke with her for ten minutes at the café. That was the first time and the LAST time she and I spoke in the past thirty-five years. Please stop making a production over nothing."

"Remember that I know you messaged her."

"I said spoke, of course we know about that incident. Which brings me to the question, what gave you the right to go on my phone anyway? I wasn't going to say anything, but you've overstepped your boundaries."

"I've overstepped my boundaries? Really? You're the one communicating with the love of your life while I'm here for you. How do you think that makes me feel?"

"Laurie, I don't know how many ways or how many times I can tell you that I am not interested in being with anyone except for you. Please stop worrying. There's nothing there."

"If you say I have nothing to worry about, I believe you. But know that I love you so much and I, too, don't know how I can spend my life without you."

Weeks went by and everything seemed to get back to normal. Laurie was smiling more. However, Frankie did start noticing that Laurie was drinking more often than usual. He noticed flasks and bottles of hard liquor dispersed around the house. He didn't want to see Laurie slip into alcoholism after the recent incident of her drinking, so he decided to confront her about her drinking.

Twenty

Areebah didn't know how to feel about Frankie. She knew he was married but it took her aback when his wife was there within minutes of them talking. If he knew she was coming, why did he not mention it to Areebah so she wouldn't be so embarrassed when she turned that corner? Other than losing her husband, that was one of the most hurtful events of her life. She was thankful to Felicia for playing it off like she was there as her support as opposed to Frankie's.

Although she didn't make a scene, it was clear that Laurie was not fooled and she could tell by looking at both Frankie's and Areebah's expressions that she was not Felicia's friend. Other than making the point that her husband is deceased, she made sure to stay out of their sights. She felt like she lost her second love.

Did she have to go another lifetime without

Frankie? Besides the fact that he was married, she began evaluating the situation and she knew that she and him couldn't be together anyway because no matter how much she cared about him, she loved Allah (SWT) the most. A Muslimah cannot marry a non-Muslim man and he never mentioned anything about accepting his Shahadah. What a dilemma Areebah found herself in. She prayed and did her best to get the thoughts of him out of her mind. She threw most of her energy into her business, which was beneficial because her net worth tripled since they spoke.

She also embossed herself within the Islamic community. She chaired many committees as well as was on the board of multiple not-for-profit Islamic organizations. Although this kept her busy, when she was home at night in bed alone, her thoughts drifted to Frankie.

"What the heck?" She thought out loud.

"I have him as a friend on the web. Let me send him a smile."

A few hours later she received a smile back from Frankie.

"Well," she posited, "he is receptive to my communication."

A few days later she decided to send him a private message. She never understood why people intended to send a private message to others on the web but posted it so all can see. Are they aware that everyone saw that post without searching for it?

"Good evening, how are you and yours?" She typed and sent.

"I'm great. We're hanging in there," he replied within minutes this time.

Areebah was beside herself when she heard the notification sound. She didn't think he would respond. She hoped this time the response was from him and not Laurie. After reading the response from him, she had to think what she should type next. She didn't want to seem too forward and disregard his marriage of thirty years and his wife. She decided that she will communicate with him but solely on a platonic platform.

"☺," was Areebah's response.

She left communication alone for a couple of days although she wanted to spend all day and all night chatting with him. She started going out to dinner with different brothers again trying to find the right man for her future husband. She even let her father suggest a few brothers for her. These brothers came from all walks of life from successful business owners to men straight from the penitentiary.

Areebah was clear regarding ex-cons; she did not want to be involved with them. That was her prerogative. A few of the brothers interested her, however, when they went for a second or third "date", she found an idiosyncrasy for each of them. It could be that she was waiting for

Frankie, but she would never admit that.

A few days later she received a notification that she had a message. She didn't feel one way or another about the notification because it was amazing how many Muslim men approached her via private message. However, when she checked her notification and saw Frankie's beautiful smile smiling at her, she was excited. She rushed to read his message.

Hey Areebah, it started. *I've been thinking of you since that day at the café. I'm sorry about the awkwardness between you and Laurie. I didn't know she was in town. As I was walking to the café, I left a message telling her to purchase the tickets. I guess she didn't want to wait for me to tell her when to come to Philly. I was happy when I saw you turn that corner in the hospital but then I remembered that my wife was standing right there. Thank you for coming to be my support. It touched my heart. Although I hadn't thought of you until I saw you in the café, I haven't stopped thinking about you since.*

Areebah read this message at least one hundred times before responding. She wanted to word her message with care because many times what one typed could be misconstrued by the written word. She didn't want to run him off while at the same time she didn't want to be the cause of his marriage disintegrating. She decided to reply to the message.

Frankie, I am so glad you messaged me. I did not want to be too forward or cause a rift in your family. When I saw you I wondered how come we never got married. I remember you telling me that you are happily married for thirty years. Although I know you said that, I thought that I would have a couple of days to spend time with you and get to know you. It was disheartening when I saw you and your wife embracing one another. But it was not my right to feel that way. I tried to not be the 'good' girl, but after I left the hospital I asked Allah (SWT) for forgiveness and decided that I do not want to be the one to break the hearts of nine people. I wish you the best in your life.

That was the hardest message Areebah ever wrote. She meant everything in the letter although she was sad to send it to him.

Twenty-One

When Frankie received the message, he was dejected. Laurie fell off the wagon again and he thought for sure he would have Areebah to talk to via the web. To top it off, Laurie was staring at him while he was looking at the computer and asked him what was wrong.

I swear, he thought to himself, if I didn't know any better, I think Laurie was bugging my computer.

"Laurie, have you bugged my computer?"

"What kind of question is that?" She deflected.

"I just thought I'd ask."

"Want to go out tonight," he wanted to go out and get some fresh air after reading that message from Areebah.

"Nah, I'll just sit here and play some games on

my phone."

He was becoming frustrated with Laurie. She did not spend quality time with him any longer. She was drinking so much that the children started to notice. The other day, Salama, who paid no attention to anyone other than herself and her friends, asked her dad why her mom was so mean. This in conjunction with Jabari always skulking around the house, it became apparent that it was time for a family meeting.

Frankie called the four children still living at the house: Jabari, Salama, Yobachi, and Chata as well as Laurie into the family room and explained that it was time for a family meeting. Yobachi and Chata were so consumed with themselves that they were unaware of any tension in the household. As long as they were able to do whatever they wanted and get whatever they needed they were okay. Jabari, on the other hand wondered why it took so long.

"Are you guys getting a divorce," Jabari said.

"Hold up! Hold up!" Frankie said. "Where'd that come from?"

"Ever since we left Philly after Grandmom's funeral, you and mom barely said two words to each other. I also saw the way that Muslim lady was looking at you," Jabari said in defense of his previous statement.

"See, even the kids noticed Areebah!" Laurie said in her drunken stupor.

"This is why I'm calling the family meeting,"

Frankie said. "First of all Laurie, you are drinking entirely too much and it's beginning to affect the kids, again. Second, Areebah is someone I grew up with and we haven't seen each other in thirty-five years except for the day I returned to Philadelphia to see my mother. Third, there is not going to be any divorce Jabari so get that thought out of your mind and that word out of your mouth."

Salama said to her mom, "It hurts me very much when I asked you for lunch money and you yelled and cursed at me. Mom, you've never done that before."

"What are you guys talking about?" Yobachi and Chata said at the same time.

Frankie had to laugh at his youngest sons. As long as they have food in their bellies; could hang out with their friends; and had all of the amenities at home, they were clueless. However, this meeting was necessary because Frankie wanted to clear the air since it appeared that Areebah did not intend on taking their friendship any further. He wasn't thinking of cheating on Laurie; but, the way Laurie's been treating him, divorce was not too far from his mind. He was surprised as to how perceptive Jabari was.

"Are we done with this 'Family Meeting'?" Laurie said showing her disdain for her husband.

"Yes Baby, but I want to speak with you privately."

"Alright children, you can go back and do

whatever it was you were doing."

"What do you want?" She said with so much vitriol that Frankie recoiled for a millisecond.

"I want US back!" He said with all sincerity and honesty.

"I want us to stop fighting or start talking because we never really discussed the subject. I want to make love to my wife without the smell of alcohol on her breath. "I want to see your beautiful smile again."

"Well, it ain't gonna happen!" She said as she grabbed her purse and her keys.

"Where are you going?" Frankie said concerned.

"I need some fresh air."

"Please just leave your purse and keys and sit out back."

"Now you're my father too?!"

"No! I love you so much and I don't want to see you hurt yourself."

"I gotta go!"

Laurie slammed the door as she left.

Twenty-Two

After Areebah responded to Frankie's message, she began feeling sad for herself. She couldn't believe that she lost another love of her life. She was furious with her mother and Inez for concocting the plan for her to meet with Frankie. Had they left well enough alone, she and Frankie would still be communicating via the web and at least she would have a part of him with her. Now regardless of what activity she engaged in, he was not far from her mind. She started to worry because she felt as if she was making him her illah, god.

Areebah began praying tahajjud, late night superogatory prayer; each night as well as performing all of the Sunnah, prayers Prophet Muhammad (PBUH) always performed outside of the obligatory prayers; and nawfl, superogatory prayers. She was always in constant supplication and remembrance of Allah (SWT); however, none of these activities stopped her thoughts and pangs for Frankie. She almost decided to marry someone else because he was showing much interest in her and he was a nice brother in the Deen (religion of Al-Islam). He had a successful business and was kind to everyone. Nevertheless, she felt that if she married him it would be under false pretenses and the brother didn't deserve that. Her dilemma of love or Deen was making her crazy.

One day she was visiting her mother and was moping around. Her mother inquired what was wrong with her. At first she said everything was okay, but the grief was getting to her that she broke down and cried.

"Ummi, why did you and Inez insist on me meeting with Frankie?"

"We thought it would be a good way for you two to reconnect."

"But he is happily married and now I feel empty and isolated without him even though I'm always around people."

"I didn't know you had feelings like that for him."

"Ummi, when Frankie got married so many years ago, I forgot about him. I never thought about him one way or the other. But, once we started talking all of the emotions we felt manifested themselves. Now I lose sleep over not being able to talk to him or to be in his life. I even considered being his second wife; and how crazy is that because he isn't a Muslim and cannot even take on a second wife."

"Sweetheart, if I knew that connecting you with Frankie would have caused so much pain for you, I never would have suggested for you to meet him."

"I know. I guess because I always kept to myself no one other than Frankie and I really knew how we felt about one another. But Ummi, one thing I've learned is that we have to accept the qadr of Allah subhana wa ta'ala. We can't say we could have or should have done anything because we are then committing shirk (associating partners with Allah). I still haven't told Abi about meeting with Frankie and he's been questioning my mood every time he sees me. What can I tell him?" Areebah said at her wits end.

"Don't worry about your Abi; I'll take care of that."

Although Areebah did not feel back to normal, she did feel better now that she was able to release some of her frustrations by talking to her mother. She tried to talk to Ra'ifah about it a few times but her response was always 'fear Allah'. Areebah did fear Allah (SWT) but that didn't stop her longing for Frankie.

She tried to befriend some of the sisters in Philly, but some sisters wanted to be her friends to either secure a job or a discount on her product. On the other hand other sisters shunned her because she was not married and they were afraid that their husbands would tell them to tell Areebah that they were interested in her. What the women did not know is that she was not interested in any of their husbands.

After talking to her mother, Areebah headed home. She forgot that she left her ringer off and she hasn't checked her phone. When she got home and looked at her phone she noticed several phone calls from Frankie.

That's odd; she thought to herself, why is Frankie calling me?

His only message was, "Call me back as soon as you receive this message."

Each time the message was the same but the sense of urgency increased. After performing salah – prayer – and getting comfortable, Areebah picked up her phone and called him. His phone was answered by his son Jabari.

"You can't even wait until my mother's body is in the ground!" He shouted and disconnected the phone.

"What is he talking about? Couldn't wait? Mother's body in the ground?"

Areebah opened her social media messenger app and private messaged Frankie.

She typed, *I just received all of your messages and I called you back. Your son Jabari answered the phone and yelled at me about not waiting and his mother's body in the ground. What happened?!*

Areebah then checked her phone to make sure

her ringer was on its highest volume and waited for Frankie's response. She wondered how Laurie died, if that is what Jabari was referring to. What did Jabari mean about not waiting until his mother's body is in the ground? For the next couple of hours Areebah was wracking her mind trying to make sense out of the multiple phone calls and cryptic messages coupled by Jabari's strong negative reaction to her.

Just as she was about to text Frankie again to ensure that he received the first message, she received a notification on her phone. What she read next stopped her dead in her tracks.

Areebah, Laurie is gone. She is no longer with us on this earth. Earlier today we had a family meeting with Laurie, the children, and me. Laurie's been drinking very heavily lately and I spoke with her about my concerns. However, she has been so hateful towards me since we left Philly and I didn't know how to bring her love back to me. Anyway, after the meeting Laurie said she was going to step out and get some fresh air.

She grabbed her purse and keys and I attempted to take the keys from her. When she wouldn't relinquish them, I then asked her, no begged her not to drive because she was very inebriated. As I was talking to her, she walked out the door and slammed the door in my face. I think I knew that she was going to drive, but after that exchange with her, I needed a breather also.

A few minutes later I heard lots of sirens. I often hear sirens around my house because I live nearby an intersection known for fatal car accidents. Initially I wasn't going to look and see what was happening. Then something inside of me told me to take a look outside. As I looked from my porch, I saw a mangled car resembling Laurie's car.

I thought to myself, 'No, this can't be Laurie.' I then went to the garage to see if she parked the car in the garage and it wasn't there. Before I knew it I was half way down the street. As I approached the crash scene, I saw the firefighters using the jaws-of-life opening up Laurie's car like a can opener. As the door fell apart in two separate pieces, I saw my wife's lifeless body in the car covered with shattered glass and blood.

I don't know what happened next, but I remember waking up to smelling salts. The police asked me if I knew the driver of the car. I replied that she was my wife. He then informed me that her alcohol level was 0.24, three times the legal limit for blood alcohol concentration. Additionally, based on eyewitness reports and the traffic cameras, your wife headed straight for the tractor trailer and never applied brakes.

Areebah, I think she committed suicide. She couldn't handle the fact that I have feelings for you. I told her in no uncertain terms that you and I have no relationship and I haven't communicated with you since we met at the café. It turns out she had spying hardware installed on all of my electronic and technological items. So when we were messaging one another she was privy to all of the messages. It seems like the messages took her over the edge.

I still can't believe that my wife is gone. By the way, I want to apologize to you regarding Jabari. He is accusing me of having an affair with you and believes this is the reason his mother is no longer with us.

He always had a sneaky suspicion that something was going on with us. At our family meeting, he addressed it to the family and made a point to say that he saw you looking at me lustfully when you thought no one was looking. This is why he's directing his anger at you rather than his mother who consciously drove her car while drunk and purposely crashed into the tractor trailer.

While reading this message, Areebah cried harder than she'd cried her entire life. She cried for being the only child. She cried for not having any close friends. She cried for losing her husband. She cried because her children would only call her on occasion. She cried because she could imagine the pain Frankie and his children were going through. To top it off, she cried because this message sounded like a goodbye message and she would not see him again even though he was no longer married and was now available for her. After clearing her soul from all of the crying, she got up the nerve to reply to Frankie.

All she wrote was, I CANNOT, WILL NOT, and SHALL NOT live another lifetime without you!!!

Although Frankie wanted to communicate with Areebah, he was guilt ridden. He wouldn't allow himself to have any pleasures in life. He blamed himself for Laurie's death. On top of that, his children were so hopeless and troubled that he didn't want to bring her into this situation yet.

A few times Jabari flat out yelled at Frankie accusing him of killing his mother. This accusation appalled Frankie but at times he felt culpable. When Jabari noticed how miserable his father was, he stopped his attacks. After a while, Frankie began to withdraw from the family activities. Although he went to work, he worked as if he was on autopilot.

Frankie's personality and outlook changed the day Laurie crashed her car into the tractor trailer. When he and Laurie were together there was incessant laughter coupled with lovingness. Frankie could not see himself enjoying laughter, ever. A few times Felicia called and he refused to speak with her or he was terse with her. She decided to fly to San Diego.

When she arrived at the house, what she saw disturbed her. This once beautiful house was rundown and it was evident that in addition to no one tending to the outside of the house, the inside was as deplorable. She decided right then and there that it was time for her to snap Frankie out of his sadness stupor.

However, once she entered the door and walked into the room where Frankie sat without moving she changed her approach. She intended to get right into his stuff and tell him to get his act together. However, after seeing his physical state and reflecting on conversations they had and understanding his mental state, she was frightened because her brother entered into deep depression.

She'd never seen him so distraught. First thing she did was clean the house. When the children arrived, she enlisted them in assisting with beautification of the house. She then began to cook food because based on the trash, they've been eating a lot of take out and she was sure they would appreciate a home cooked meal. With compassion, she encouraged him to shower and put on some fresh clothes.

Because she had bouts of depression in the past, she understood the signs. She anticipated that he was in a depression based on their phone conversations and reports from the children. But what she observed solidified her presumption. She decided to take it upon herself to guide him to get the help he needed. The first step was him showering and putting on fresh clothes.

Although showering and getting dressed does not cure depression, she knew that once he got up he would feel a little better. When Frankie came back downstairs, she motioned for him to come into the kitchen where she was cooking.

"Hey Big Brother," she said with a forced smile on her face.

"Hey Sis," he said with no interest in speaking with her.

"What are you doing here?"

"Well, every time I called you we only spoke for a minute, maybe two. Other times you flat out refused to speak to me. Then I spoke with Jabari and he told me how you were moping around the house, not showing interest in anything, allowing the children do whatever they wanted to do and to top it off, not showering. So, I figured it was my duty as your sister to come here and whip you into shape," she said attempting to put joviality into the situation.

Frankie didn't smile or laugh. He just stood there staring into space. It was at this time that Felicia knew that he needed professional help. She contemplated on how to introduce the subject to her brother. She didn't want to sound condescending but she also did not want to be a pushover where he thought he could say everything was okay and she would leave and go back to Philly. She decided to just start with the most obvious statement.

"Frankie," she said speaking with caution.

"You're in a deep depression and I'm worried about you."

"I'm just mourning Laurie," he said trying to sound a little upbeat now.

"This is more than mourning Laurie."

"Laurie's been dead over six months and although I am not putting a time limit on mourning, your actions fall into the realm of depression. For example, you do the bare minimum to take care of your children and you are not taking care of yourself any longer. Besides just now, when was the last time someone had to remind you to bathe?

"The Frankie I knew was so concerned about his appearance that sometimes he would take two or three showers per day."

"I am feeling a little sadder than expected. And if I'm honest, it has a lot more to do than just losing Laurie. It's like I lost my two loves on that fatal day."

"I understand. I've seen Areebah a few times and although she isn't looking as bad as you, she has sadness in her eyes. If you want to be with her, it definitely cannot be possible if you don't shower and take care of yourself."

"Okay, what do you suggest?"

"Does your company have any type of services that help with mental health?"

"They may. I think I overheard some coworkers talking about it recently but I pulled away from communicating with anyone so I'm not sure."

"Well, your first task is to get on the phone and call HR for your company and ask them if you are covered for mental health coverage."

"Okay."

Frankie retrieved his phone and called the HR Department. The HR Manager stated that they have coverage for mental health and she was happy that he reached out to her. Everyone at the office was concerned about his withdrawal from everything. This made him reflect on the conversations by his coworkers. Maybe when they were having the conversation about mental health coverage they were talking to him but he was so far gone that he was unaware. He returned to the kitchen to let his sister know what he learned.

"Yes, they do offer mental health. As a matter of fact, they were waiting for me to request assistance."

"Was I really that bad off?"

"Was?" She said smiling. "Am should be the verb of choice."

He thought to himself, how could I let myself get this low? Just a year ago Laurie and I were so in love with one another. We couldn't wait to be together and we couldn't keep our hands off of each other. Now she is no longer on this earth. I guess it is time for me to take the first step and get some help.

Felicia remained with them for a few days but had to return home to take care of her family and to get back to work. She was happy to see the positive changes in her brother's outlook. She knew he had a difficult year. First their mother died and then his wife. The straw that broke the camel back was his guilt he felt for thinking about Areebah that he cut off all contact with her.

"Well," she said to him, "it looks like you are on the road to recovery."

"I love you and the kids Frankie. Do not hesitate to call if you ever have anything you want to talk about, happy or sad."

"I love you too Baby Sis. Have a safe trip. If

you happen to run into Areebah, let me know if she still thinks about me."

"I sure will. Well, I better go because I have to return the car and make it to the terminal. Love Ya."

Frankie was happy to see Felicia leave. Now that he was out of his stupor, he wanted to login to the web to see if Areebah sent him any messages. He did miss talking to her and seeing her beautiful smile.

Is that a tinge of happiness I feel? Maybe I am on the road to recovery.

Twenty-Three

I still can't believe Laurie died, Areebah thought to herself.

Although Areebah tried to feel bad that Laurie died, she felt this was a sign from Allah (SWT) that it was meant for her and Frankie to get together.

All he had to do now was take his Shahadah, she mused to herself.

Others may call her cold-blooded because of her feelings regarding Laurie's death, but she figured since she never knew her and Laurie was the obstacle between her and Frankie that it was good riddance.

One person's sadness is another's joy, she theorized.

However, using the façade she was famous for, Areebah never let anyone know her true feelings regarding Laurie and Frankie. Whenever her mother mentioned it to her, Areebah put on the performance of a lifetime.

"Inna illahi wa inna ilaihi raji'un (verily from Allah we come and to Him we return)," She said after her mother started talking about Laurie's death.

"May Allah (SWT) make it easy for Frankie and his children," she continued. But, in the back of her mind she was also thinking that may Allah (SWT) make it easy for her and Frankie to finally be together. She tried a few times to communicate with Frankie via social media but he never responded to her messages. She also noticed that he was not posting on the web at all any longer.

She even made it a point to find out where Felicia was so she could "accidentally" bump into her so she could inquire about Frankie. The last time she saw Felicia she asked about him.

"Frankie's not in a good place right now," she said looking down at her feet.

"He's fallen into a deep depression. He's not taking care of himself or his children. I just returned from visiting him and helping him and the children. I even told him that you asked about him to see if that would enliven his spirits. He just continued to stare out into space. I am really concerned about my brother."

Areebah did not like what she heard. There had to be a way to help him.

She went back home and began plotting on how to get Frankie to communicate with her. To her surprise, when she opened her laptop and logged into the web, she was surprised to see a private message from Frankie.

Hey Areebah, I know I fell off the face of the earth and stopped communicating with you, but I felt responsible for Laurie's death. Although we haven't communicated since we met at the café, I've thought about you often. Prior to Laurie dying in the car crash, she and I had a serious talk and I knew she was in a bad place. I did my best to love her and not think of you. However, between her drinking and her anger, she refused any goodness I offered her. Although I've never admitted this to anyone and this is the first time what I am about to type left my mind, I was planning on leaving Laurie if she didn't stop drinking and started being kinder to me. However, I never ever wanted to see her dead.

Her death was hard on my children; Jabari was affected the most since he blamed me for his mother's death. Not only did he blame me, he also blamed you. He said if you didn't show up at the funeral his mother never would have felt threatened. I tried to let him know you had nothing to do with it, but Jabari is stubborn and when he gets a thought in his head, only he can change his thoughts.

Felicia was just down here and she told me you asked about me. Although I appeared uninterested, upon hearing your name and knowing that you still cared for me brought me out of my depression. Well, I'm not totally out of the dark yet; however, hearing your name and then logging onto the web and seeing your face really made life a little more bearable. I love you Areebah and I want us to be together.

Areebah was shocked at this message. Here she was plotting for a way to get Frankie to communicate with her and when she went online, waiting in her private message was the beginning of her du'a being answered.

"Alhamdulillah (All praises belong to Allah)!"

"Allahu Akbar (Allah is the greatest)!"

Areebah always believed that Allah (SWT) answered all du'a. So she was thankful to Allah (SWT) and made two Sunnah rakat to thank Him for answering her du'a. She knew that this was only the beginning and that there was a lot of work to do; nevertheless, it was promising because Frankie reached out to her first.

Although she was not desperate and had ample opportunities to get married, the only other man she wanted to marry besides Murad was Frankie. Even though she would never verbalize this fact to her mother or father, she didn't want to be married to someone else when the opportunity for her to marry Frankie presented itself. Speaking with her mom throughout the day, she never mentioned the message from Frankie to her mother. This was one memory she wanted to cherish with just the two of them.

After about an hour, Areebah decided to sit down and respond to Frankie's message. She wanted to make sure that Frankie knew that she was interested in him but she did not want to sound insensitive. She took her time to respond so that Frankie would be interested in continuing communication with her.

Frankie, I am so glad to hear from you. I was concerned when you stopped communicating with me. I became more concerned when I didn't see you communicating on the web at all. Felicia told me that you were in a deep depression. I am so glad that hearing my name and seeing my face helped some of the depression wash away. ☺ If ever you need someone to talk to for a laugh or a cry, please remember that I am here for you. I am so sorry about the guilt you feel for Laurie's death; nonetheless, it wasn't your fault. You were a great husband and you were doing what you were supposed to do for your family.

I cannot lie, I was ecstatic when I saw your message. Although I was not in a deep depression, I was miserable because I was looking forward to chatting with you. Well, I have to go and I'll be anxiously awaiting your reply. ☺"

After reading over the message, Areebah changed it a few times and decided on the previous draft before deciding to send it. Although she was happy with the message, she then toyed with the idea of not sending it. She clicked on various tabs in the internet browser; finally winning her jihad of the nafs (struggle of the soul), she decided to click send.

"Well, the ball's in his court now," she rationalized.

Areebah's day turned out better than she planned. She decided to go see her parents; she had to see her mother. She was excited and wanted to share the latest information about her and Frankie with her mother. She was aware that despite the fact that her mother wanted her to forget about him; but she also knew that her mother would be excited to hear that he was still interested in her. Of course she would bring this conversation up when her father was not around. The idea of his daughter marrying a kaffir was repulsive to him.

"As salaamu alaikum," Areebah said greeting the house as she entered.

"Wa laikum mus salaam," her parents replied in unison.

"We're in the family room, come join us," her mother said.

"What do we owe the pleasure of seeing our baby girl today?" Her father said.

"I am having such a wonderful day that I figured it was a great time to visit my parents."

"That's wonderful. What makes this day so wonderful?" Her father said.

"Allah subhana wa ta'ala allowed me to wake up and seek His forgiveness for another day. Isn't that enough?" She said while hugging her parents.

"Well, I am happy to see you regardless of what brings you here."

Kashifah sat quiet and mused at the banter between her husband and their daughter. She thought there was much more to Areebah's jovial disposition than she was saying.

"Honey, will you go out and buy Areebah and

me some water ices and mustard pretzels? It is such a warm day today and that is a great way for us to cool down," Kashifah asked Shafaat wanting to get to the real reason Areebah was so happy.

"For my ladies, anything!" He said as he grabbed the keys and headed out the door.

"Alright, what is really making you happy?" Kashifah said as soon as she heard the car leave the driveway.

"Ummi," Areebah began almost shouting, "Frankie reached out to me today."

"Really? How?" Kashifah said waiting with abated breath for the next words from Areebah.

"He's been in a very bad depression and he couldn't cope after Laurie died. However, his sister went to visit him last week and she told him I asked about him. He said that is what helped begin the healing process."

"Alhamdulillah!" Kashifah said.

"In shaa Allah, Allah subhana wa ta'ala will guide him to Al-Islam and we can get married. But honestly Ummi, I would even consider marrying him whether he is Muslim or not."

"Areebah, don't let Shaitan whisper in your ears or heart. Regardless of what you feel in your heart, you have to abide by what Allah subhana wa ta'ala said regarding whom we can and cannot marry."

"I understand that Ummi. But, none of these brothers out here are good for me. All of them have ulterior motives. Either they want me to be their third or fourth wife and take care of all of their children. Or they are 'entrepreneurs' and need a place to live and their 'Khadijah' (older woman with money). There are a few good ones, but they are looking for someone willing to have a child. Both of my children are grown and I am not interested in having any babies at this age."

"Areebah, Sweetie, I really do understand. But, how do you think your father will react to you marrying a non-Muslim?"

"What are you talking about her marrying a non-Muslim?" Shafaat shouted as he heard the end of their conversation.

"No daughter of mine will marry a kafir. Is that what made you come here in such a happy mood? A kafir? And Kashifah, you knew that was why she was here and you sent me out to so you two can talk? Here, take your water ices and pretzels. You two wanted to be alone, then as salaamu alaikum." Thrusting the water ices and pretzels towards them, Kashifah grabbed them before they fell as Shafaat stormed away.

"Abi," Areebah said with respect and determination, "you walked in on the end of the conversation. I am not planning on marrying a kafir. In shaa Allah he will take his Shahadah prior to us getting married."

"So, who is this kafir? How long have you been seeing him?"

"I haven't been seeing him. We just recently

began communicating again. It's Frankie."

Shafaat sat down as if all of the wind was knocked out of him. He looked back and forth from Areebah to Kashifah. They in turn became silent and looked at one another.

"I should have known. I tried all your life to keep the two of you apart. He is not a Muslim and I wish you didn't even attend Inez's funeral. It's not like she was a Muslim. That is what probably gave you the idea of communicating with him in the first place."

Areebah and Kashifah looked at each other for a brief moment hoping Shafaat didn't see their eyes grow wide at his words. Both of them still held the secret about the time they set up a way for Frankie to run into Areebah before Inez passed away. Both women agreed that it was best to keep that secret between the two of them.

"Abi, you're so upset because he is a kafir, why didn't you just give him dawah (invitation to Islam) instead of keeping us apart?"

"It wasn't my responsibility to give him dawah."

"Wasn't it?" Areebah asked as she and Kashifah looked at each other confuzzled – confused and puzzled.

"I disagree Abi. One responsibility of the Muslim is to invite others to the Deen. Anyway, maybe he would have taken his Shahadah back then. You just don't like him and the best way to keep him away from me was not to teach him about Islam."

"Areebah, I will not allow you to disrespect me in my house."

"I am not disrespecting you Abi; but, I am grown with children and grandchildren and I am able to make my own decisions. I know that it is haram (forbidden) for me to marry someone that is not Muslim; but Allah subhana wa ta'ala answers all du'a and I made sincere du'a that Allah subhana wa ta'ala guides him to this Deen. If he does accept his Shahadah and asks me to marry him, I will be marrying him, bi ithni Allah (with Allah's permission)."

Areebah was neither emotional nor angry when she explained this to her father. She spoke to her father in the same manner in which she spoke to her customers and employees. She was an intelligent woman and who knew her Deen. She will not let anyone tell her how to live her life. She felt herself succumbing to sad and angry feelings. Before allowing those emotions to take over, she decided it was time to go.

"Well, I have some more errands to run. I love you all and I'll see you again soon."

"As salaamu alaikum."

"Wa laikum mus salaam, Sweetie," her mother said.

"Wa laikum mus salaam," said her father as he sat brooding.

Twenty-Four

"How long have you known about her and Frankie communicating?" Shafaat asked disappointed in his wife.

"For a little while."

"And you didn't inform me?"

"I didn't know that I had to inform you of everyone our grown daughter communicates with."

"Maybe not everyone, but definitely Frankie."

"Why Frankie?" Kashifah wanted to know why Shafaat was always against Frankie.

"I don't want to talk about it," he said as he stormed out the room.

Twenty-Five

Frankie took his sister's and HR manager's advice and made an appointment to see a psychologist. After telling the psychologist about his father's incarceration; his mother's death; and his wife's death in addition to him finding and losing his first love Frankie began to feel a little weight lift off his shoulders. The psychologist explained to Frankie that because he kept his feelings in for so long that when Laurie died and he stopped communicating with Areebah that his mind began feeling as if everything was lost although he still had his children and grandchild that loved and needed him.

Frankie decided that he would continue seeing the psychologist while making improvements to his house and spending more time with his children and grandchild. Although Frankie reached out to Areebah after Felicia left, he did not communicate with her for a while after that. He did, however, read and reread her reply to his message. He was not sure if he was ready to take the plunge with Areebah.

He knew that he wanted to be with her; however, his children needed him and he needed to improve his mental health. He also knew that the one thing that would hold Areebah back from being with him was him not being Muslim. Prior to Laurie dying, Frankie began reading the Qur'an – the Holy Scripture read by Muslims. He didn't know if it was because he saw Areebah again or if his perspective changed, however, he did know that he was more receptive to what he read in the Qur'an.

Frankie was never one for organized religion. However, after the past year, he was well aware that there is a being greater than him. In addition, he was interested in forging a relationship with Areebah that would end in marriage and he knew what the biggest deal breaker was. He did not, on the other hand, want to enter into a way of life for anyone except for himself. So, without informing Areebah of his actions, he began studying Islam.

In addition to reading the Qur'an, he remembered seeing posts from many of his Muslim friends of different lecturers on Islam. So he went online in search of some videos and typed in Islam and Muslim. He found so many interesting videos that he consumed them like someone who was without food or water for weeks.

He logged onto the web three or four times per day and joined many Islamic groups. Since there were cookies enabled on his internet browser, many suggestions appeared and Frankie joined more and more Islamic groups. He liked many of these pages. Quotes from the Qur'an and Hadith as well as Islamic scholars began to fill his newsfeed. He was surprised of the content he read.

Whether he and Areebah ever got together or not, he was determined to learn more about Islam. One day he decided to go to the local masjid. He happened to go on a Saturday evening. That particular Saturday evening the masjid was having its family night. Frankie was surprised to see the diversity at the masjid.

Being from Philly, there are multitudes of Muslims. However, of the multitudes, ninety percent that are seen are African-American. But when he stepped foot in this masjid and he was welcomed and encouraged to sit and listen to the lecture, he was overwhelmed. Then, after the lecture, they offered him to stay and eat. This is nothing like he expected a masjid to be.

Although the women and men were separated, there was no struggle over the women being in the front of the masjid. Moreover, everyone seemed to be happy and okay with sitting on the floor to listen to the lecture as well as sitting together outside to eat without fanfare for the imam.

The more he studied and attended the masjid, the more he knew the time for him to take his Shahadah will come. However, he wanted to take his time and he did not want anyone to know what he was doing. His children noticed a difference in him, though. They also realized that he stopped drinking and no longer bought pork for the household.

"Daddy," Salama said, "is that Muslim woman moving here?"

"Why do you ask?" Frankie was surprised by the question from his daughter.

Although he thought about Areebah often, he communicated on rare occasions with her since learning more about the Deen. He wanted everything to be done the halal (permitted) way.

"No, I haven't spoken with her in a while. What made you ask that question?"

"You stopped drinking. You don't buy any pork anymore. One time when I was on your computer, I saw a site up with a Muslim man on it. I also caught you reading the Qur'an a couple of times."

"Well, I am going to be honest with you. Areebah is someone that I knew since we were younger than you are now. She and I always had chemistry and always liked one another. However, things always seemed to get in the way.

When she and I went away to school we lost contact. I forgot about her until the day I saw her at a café when I was visiting your grandmother."

"So, mom was right. You were planning on leaving her for Areebah?"

"No, not at all, I loved your mom with all my heart. I think she sensed something between Areebah and me. However, nothing ever happened between the two of us. We hardly spoke during those times your mother was upset."

"But, are you planning on moving her into my mom's house?!"

"First of all, this is my house. Second of all, your mom's been dead over a year and I am a man. I have a right to be happy and I have a right to choose who I am happy with."

"Regarding my decision on Al-Islam, that has nothing to do with Areebah. Yes, initially I started reading the Qur'an because I know that she is not interested in marrying anyone who is not Muslim. However, after reading the Qur'an; listening to multiple lecturers; and visiting the masjid a few times; when I make my mind up, it will be because I want to do it and not because I want to be with a woman."

"But Dad, we are just getting you back. We missed you all of those months. Now you want to bring someone else into our family?" Salamah said at the brink of crying. One huge crocodile tear hung at the precipice of her bottom eyelid as she wrung her hands trying to control her emotions.

"Baby Girl, I love you very much. Don't be sad. When your mother was here I loved her a lot. But, she will not come back. It is not fair for me to go the rest of my life alone."

"Let me ask you this question. Do you have a boyfriend?"

"Yes."

"Are you planning on going away to college?"

"Yes"

"Do your brothers have girlfriends?"

"Yes."

"Do you all go out many nights and not come back until midnight?"

"Yes."

"So, while you all are out having fun, you want me to sit in this quiet, lonesome house by myself?"

"Well…"

"And you want me to look at your mother's picture and remember what things were before she started drinking? You want me to live on a memory of a lifetime ago? I love Areebah and when I'm ready, I AM going to ask her to marry me?"

"But I don't think it's the right time."

"Thank you for your concern Salamah, but this matter is not up for discussion and the conversation ends now!"

Salamah stomped out of the room incensed. She couldn't wait to talk to her brothers. If her father decided to marry this Areebah person, then she will make her life a living hell. She entered her room and began planning the evil actions she intended to put Areebah through whenever she moved into HER mother's house.

Although Frankie didn't like speaking harsh to his daughter, he did feel the need to get his feelings out in the open. As a matter of fact, after he and Salamah spoke, he felt better than he had since he found out about his mother's illness. Frankie was convinced; he loved Areebah and was ready to spend the remainder of his life with her.

The next Friday Frankie decided to see what a Jumuah, Friday congregational prayer, looked like. He headed to the masjid and went to observe the prayer. He was surprised at the amount of people who attended the masjid. When he came to the masjid a few Saturdays he saw a lot of Muslims. But, this crowd was triple the size of the crowd on Saturday.

People of all walks of life came into the masjid and sat on the floor. Did you hear that, the floor! There were some who sat in chairs, they appeared to be old or injured. But, for the most part, all of the congregants sat on the floor for about thirty minutes to hear the imam speak.

There was no singing, dancing, music, just a short and to the point lecture. They then stood to

pray. After they prayed, some people rushed to
their cars to get back to work while others stayed
and prayed more. Then there were those that
hung around to talk, eat, and congregate to build
their brotherhood and sisterhood; which by the
way, the women remained in the back of the
masjid and were not up in the men's face. This
was nothing that he expected.

He decided to take that day off from work
because he was not sure how long Jumuah lasted.
So he decided to use a vacation day. He thought
the day of worship was like the Christians and
Jewish people where they have a Sabbath and
cannot work on their Sabbath. When Frankie
mentioned this to one of the Muslim men he told
him:

"We pray five times every day. The Friday
prayer, al-Jumuah, is just one of our prayers
changed to be a congregational prayer with a
lecture. However, we still go back to work. The
Muslims do not have a Sabbath."

Since Frankie was listening to many lecturers
on internet radio as well as watching numerous
Islamic scholars on the web, he was aware of
praying five times a day but the Jumuah prayer
surprised him. Frankie wanted to meet with the
imam and he thought it would be difficult to
meet with him, but within fifteen minutes, most
of the congregants were gone and instead of him
searching out the imam, the imam approached
him.

"As salaamu alaikum."

"I'm not Muslim."

"I've seen you here a few times. Are you interested in becoming Muslim?"

"I am! After all I've seen today, I am even more amazed with Al-Islam. I know I have to take the Shahadah, but what exactly does that mean?"

"First, did you take a shower and shampoo your hair prior to coming here today?"

"Yes."

"Next, do you believe that there is only one God and He has no son or partners?"

"When I was growing up I never had a religion. However, sometimes my grandmother would take me to her church. When we were in there, I could never understand why they had to pray through a man to get to God. So, yes, I do believe that He has no son or partners."

"Alhamdulillah. That means all the praises belong to Allah."

"Do you believe in all of the prophets from Adam to Muhammad including Jesus as a prophet; Moses, Aaron, Abraham, and Jacob?"

"Absolutely!"

"Well, you're ready to take your Shahadah. Prior to you taking this huge step, I want to let you know that it is easy becoming a Muslim. Staying a Muslim is when the difficulties arrive. The Shaitan, devil, hates when he loses one of his foot soldiers so he comes to you from the front and the back; from the left and the right; and from the top and the bottom. Therefore, be aware that being a Muslim will not be all happy go lucky. You will have people from your family; people you've loved your entire life going against you and trying to make you feel bad for your decision. So, after knowing all of that, are you still interested in reciting the kalimah Shahadah?"

"Yes sir."

"As salaamu alaikum brothers and sisters, there is a brother here who wants to take his Shahadah. Please, if you do not need to leave right away, please stay and witness his Shahadah."

"Okay, repeat after me in Arabic."

"Ash hadu an la ilaha il-Allah."

"Ash hadu an la ilaha il-Allah."

"Wa ash hadu 'anna Muhammadar Rasul lullah."

"Wa ash hadu 'anna Muhammadar Rasul lullah."

"Now repeat after me in English"

"I bear witness that there is no god but Allah."

"I bear witness that there is no god but Allah."

"And I bear witness that Muhammad is the Messenger of Allah."

"And I bear witness that Muhammad is the Messenger of Allah."

"Takbir (exclaim)!" The imam said.

"Allahu Akbar (Allah is the Greatest)!" The congregation replied.

"Takbir!"

"Allahu Akbar!"

"Takbir!"

"Allahu Akbar!"

Frankie was elated with his decision. The only members of his family he was concerned about regarding him taking his Shahadah were his children. Since his mother passed, Frankie didn't communicate with his extended family as much and their opinions did not affect his life one way or the other.

"Well, on to stage two," Frankie said to himself.

Twenty-Six

Frankie hadn't communicated with Areebah since the message explaining his condition except for occasional hellos and how is your day. Areebah felt positive and nervous. She felt positive because Frankie was coming out of his depression and it was because his sister told him she was asking about him. She was nervous because there has been no substantive communication from him since the message. However, Areebah believed that her du'as always came to light and she believed that the qadr of Allah (SWT) was for her and Frankie to be together.

In addition to Areebah's mixed emotions, her father was still upset with her because of her stance for Frankie. A few times Areebah stopped by her parents' house to check on them and to hang out with them and her father returned her greetings and then got up out of his chair and went into another part of the house.

"He's been that way since the day he found out about Frankie. He speaks to me from bare necessity."

"In shaa Allah, he'll come around. However, I do mean what I said. It is my life. I've been married; have children and grandchildren; and am now widowed. I deserve some more happiness in my life. Frankie and I will build that happiness together."

"When was the last time you spoke with him?"

"I've heard from him occasionally."

"And you believe that you two will be together?" Her mother said as she looked for sanity in her daughter.

"I trust and believe in Allah subhana wa ta'ala and I believe he answers du'a."

"Just from the short conversations I had with Frankie, he is not a man to jump into situations. It is possible that as we speak he is learning about Al-Islam. Back when we were little kids and teenagers, I always told Frankie that I cannot marry anyone who is not Muslim. I also reiterated that when I saw him at the café. Therefore, I trust that Allah subhana wa ta'ala is in control and everything will work out as planned."

"Okay Sweetheart," her mother said concerned about her daughter's mental health.

"Well Ummi, I have to go now. I'll be by to

see you again. Maybe Abi will stop hating me."

"He doesn't hate you. He doesn't like that you and I were keeping secrets from him. He felt left out of the loop."

"Okay."

As Areebah was leaving her parents' house, she thought about what her mother said. She did need to let her father in on the plans. He was her father and when she gets married he will be her wali/wakil - guardian. Trying not to focus on what her mother said regarding Frankie not contacting her. She had faith in Allah (SWT). However, she remembered the Hadith that says, "Pray but remember to tie your camel."

When she arrived home, she made a beeline to her desk. On the desk was her laptop computer. She opened her laptop and logged onto the web. There still was no reply from Frankie. She decided to write him another message inquiring about his health and children.

"Hey Frankie, how have you been? I haven't heard from you in a while. Are you and the children doing well? I was thinking about a trip to San Diego. Are you up for a visitor? I've never been there it would be great to see that area. Let me know if you're doing well.

"Well, I tied my camel," she thought happy with what she did.

"Now I just have to wait for him to respond. If he doesn't respond within a week, then maybe I misread the signals from the message," she thought to herself trying not to get depressed.

She began preparing for a trip to San Diego. Certain that Frankie would welcome her with open arms; she searched the web for places to go while in San Diego. The first place she would go was La Jolla. She loved the water and whenever she was in a coastal city she always visited the beach. After reading that La Jolla has the most beautiful coastline in San Diego she decided that was where she will visit multiple times.

While searching the web and daydreaming about her trip to San Diego, she heard the notification. (Although she was surfing the web, she always kept the notification window open just in case Frankie responded to her message.) She minimized the window that she was reading about La Jolla and went to her notification page. She was happy to see the notification was a reply to her message from Frankie.

However, what she read was bittersweet.

"Hey Areebah, I have been busy and you are still on my mind. Do not lose hope. I am still interested in us. However, I do not think now is a good time for you to come down here. Now, I cannot stop you from coming to visit. But, I will not be able to see you at this time. The children and I are doing much better. We are still working past Laurie's death and my depression. I'll try to contact you more frequently. Take care."

"What?" She screamed to no one in particular.

She was confused and did not know what to

take from the message.

I understand about him wanting to get him and his children on the right foot again since he was in such a depression. But, how come he doesn't want me to come to San Diego?

"Okay, thank you for the quick response."

That's all Areebah could think to reply at the time. She was not expecting the message she received. However, after rereading the reply, Areebah wasn't too upset. He did type that he still wanted "us". That was promising. She decided that she was being too forceful and it was only fair for him to get right with himself and his children prior to bringing someone else into the mix.

Twenty-Seven

What she did not know was that Frankie just took his Shahadah and wanted to do everything in accordance of Al-Islam. He did not want her to come to San Diego until they were ready to be husband and wife. Moreover, he was in the process of letting his children know about his acceptance of Al-Islam and his decision to marry her.

"What do you really know about her?" Jabari said.

"It's been thirty-five years since the two of you really spent time together. Are you going to marry her without taking time to know her?"

"While I am going to take the time to get to know her, we are in our late forties and it does not make any sense to go years trying to "get to know" someone."

"But Dad," Salamah began, "how can you let someone take Mom's place?"

"She is not taking your mom's place. What we have has nothing to do with your mom and me. Also, it's going on two years since your mom passed and we had this conversation before Salamah."

"Does she know that you became a Muslim?" Yobachi said.

"No she doesn't. I want to let her know that when I speak with her, not through a message on the web."

"Dad, if this is what you want and it makes you happy, then I support you 100%," said Chata.

"Thank you son, that makes me feel much better. Jabari and Salama, I know this is difficult for you two, but think about it, I deserve companionship and happiness just like all of you have."

"Okay Dad," they all said in unison.

Twenty-Eight

Meanwhile, building from the "us" in the message, Areebah felt it was time for her to talk to her children about Frankie. She never introduced any of the brothers that were interested in her to her children. It was not necessary. But she had a feeling that she and Frankie would get married soon and now is the time to let her children know.

Her two children, Sahlah and Baqir, have been concerned about their mother since their father died. Sahlah worked in Dubai as a project manager for a major Fortune 500 company and doesn't have much time to visit her mother.

Baqir, Areebah's youngest child, had many ups and downs in his life. He had a daughter and a girlfriend and he didn't come around or call his mother often because he didn't feel like being lectured to by her. Baqir decided to move to North Dakota because there were a lot of job opportunities there and their rate of pay was higher than many other states.

Sahlah called Areebah every week. However, Baqir was sporadic with his phone calls. Many times they were coupled with requests for money. When they do call, they check up on her to see if she's okay. Their mother was very private and put on a good façade.

However, during the past few phone calls, she sounded happy. One time Baqir called his grandfather and he was rambling about some kafir. It wasn't making any sense because his mother was not one to give audience to a kafir.

Areebah called Sahlah first.

"As salaamu alaikum Sahlah."

"Wa laikum mus salaam Ummi. Kayfahalik (How are you)?"

"Bi khair (I'm well), Alhamdulillah. Wa ante (and you)?"

"Bi khair."

"How have you been Sweetie?" Areebah said.

"I'm well. I am truly enjoying myself here in Al Ain. Although women wear the niqab (face covering) and jilbab (long covered dress), there are so many activities for women. Work is also going quite well. How are you Ummi?"

"I am quite fine. I have something important to tell you."

"Is this about the kafir Baqir was telling me

about?"

"What?" Areebah said surprised to hear that question.

"What are you talking about?"

"Baqir told me that Grandpop said you were interested in marrying some kafir that you knew a long time ago."

"Well, I am interested in marrying a friend from a long time ago. At this time he is not Muslim but he is studying the Deen," Areebah said lying because she hadn't communicated with Frankie in a while and she didn't know what he was doing.

"That is what I wanted to talk to you about. He has eight children and one grandchild. Four of his children live with him. His wife died two years ago in a horrible car crash. He's a nice person and I made du'a and istikhara (prayer seeking answers from Allah) recently and I believe that Allah subhana wa ta'ala answers all du'a."

"But Ummi, how long and how many times have you told me not to try to 'convert a brother'?"

"I am not setting out to 'convert a brother'."

"It just seems hypocritical. This is one of the reasons that I am not married today. I've met many men who were interested in me as well as willing to learn more about the Deen. But each time I sought your counsel, you reminded me that it is best to marry a man who is already Muslim. What changed?"

"I am not being hypocritical. It is possible that during the times you sought my counsel I was still married to your father and I wasn't knowledgeable about the struggles of many Muslimahs. However, I really think you will like him."

"I don't think so. But any way, I am half way around the world so I don't have to be in his presence. Before making a final decision, reflect on who a Muslimah should marry."

"You don't have to remind me about who a Muslim should marry. I understand your anger and frustration and in shaa Allah one day you'll understand. However, don't be too upset with me, this is something that I believe is the qadr of Allah."

"Well Ummi, I really do wish you happiness. It's been a while since Abi died and I always wanted you to be happy. In shaa Allah this man will accept Al-Islam and this conversation will be all academic."

"JazakAllah khair (May Allah award you a lot) for the good words, I love you. Ma salaama. I have to go now."

"Ma salaama Ummi, I love you too."

After disconnecting the phone from Sahlah, Areebah replayed the conversation in her head. Why would her father talk to her children about her? Why even mention Frankie? If he was that upset, why didn't he call and talk to her? Why focus so much on Frankie being a kafir? Was

Sahlah right? Was I being hypocritical?

She never thought she was being hypocritical. The advice she gave Sahlah she meant. When Murad was alive and they were so happy, she never thought about having to find another husband. The advice she gave Sahlah was from twenty-five years ago. Is she the reason her daughter has yet to get married? These revelations made her have trepidations about her relationship between Frankie and herself.

The dilemma between love or Deen was really beginning to bother Areebah. She considered messaging Frankie and telling him that if he doesn't accept his Shahadah that they cannot become an "us", but it seemed so difficult for her. Before messaging Frankie, she decided to call Baqir.

"As salaamu alaikum Baqir."

"Wa laikum mus salaam."

"Have you spoken with Sahlah?"

"Yes, I just got off the phone with her. She told me that you were interested in some guy. Is this the same guy Grandpop was telling me about, the kafir?"

"Na'am (yes)."

"Well Ummi, is he a kafir?"

"A kafir is someone who doesn't believe in Allah. No, he is not a kafir; he is just in the state of jahaliyah (ignorance)."

"Ummi, stop playing semantics, is he Muslim?"

"Laa, he isn't Muslim."

"And you're really considering marrying him? What's going on here? Can you not find a good Muslim man?"

"There are many good Muslim men. However, after praying and trusting in Allah, I really believe that he will accept his Shahadah and we will get married."

"In shaa Allah Ummi. I know that this has to be difficult for you. You've always made good decisions and I will be here to support you whenever you need it."

"Shukran Son. I truly appreciate that."

"Well, I have to go now. I love you and I'll talk to you soon. As salaamu alaikum."

"Wa laikum mus salaam Son and I love you as well."

Twenty-Nine

"I'll be flying into Philadelphia in a week," Frankie informed his children.

"I'm going to ask Areebah to marry me."

"Seriously," Salamah said on the brink of crying as she yelled.

"Yes, she is concerned because I haven't communicated with her and she doesn't know that I took my Shahadah."

"But, I'm not ready for you to get married yet," Salamah protested.

"Salamah, I love you. But this has nothing to do with you. I'm doing this for myself. It is not up for discussion."

"Well Dad, are you bringing her back here to live with us?" Jabari said.

"I'm not sure. She is a successful woman up in Philadelphia and I don't know what her ultimate plans are. When I know, I'll let you all know."

"Dad, I just want you to be happy," said Yobachi smiling.

"Me too, this is the happiest I've seen you since Mom died. If Areebah can make you happy, then I'm all for it," Chata said.

"Okay, well we'll have more than enough time to discuss this; I am not leaving until next week."

As the children went to their respective rooms, Frankie began to wonder if what he was doing was right. Areebah did message him and in no uncertain terms, left all the cards in his hands; however, he never responded.

What if she was tired of his lack of communication? Frankie pushed the negative thoughts to the back of his mind. He didn't want his depression to reveal its ugly head. He finalized the airplane ticket; rental car; and hotel reservations. When he arrived in Philadelphia, he planned on going to her parents' house first to speak with her father. He knew for years that Shafaat didn't like him but now that he was grown and Muslim, he felt it was only right to talk to him man to man.

The week went by in a flash. Between packing and making sure the children had food in the house as well as reviewing with Jabari the schedule for his siblings, Frankie was busy. He also had to close projects he had at work that were coming up the current and following weeks. This is the busiest Frankie recalled being in a long time, and he loved it!

A week later Frankie headed to the airport. Instead of parking in the long term parking lot, Jabari drove him to the airport. He also requested Salamah, Yobachi, and Chata to ride along. The ride took about forty-five minutes. This gave Frankie time to speak with the children and reassure them that everything would be fine and they would grow to love Areebah. Yobachi and Chata looked at each other and smiled while Jabari and Salamah seethed with anger.

"When I land in Philadelphia, I'll group text all of you to let you know I arrived. If there are any problems, call me."

"Okay Dad," Jabari said longing for his mother.

Thirty

Salamah refused to look at her father. She still couldn't believe that he was marrying the woman responsible for her mother's death. She didn't care what her dad said; she knew Areebah was the cause of her no longer having her mom.

She will pay for this! Salamah thought to herself as she began concocting a plan to get Areebah back for causing Laurie's death.

Once they arrived home, Salamah rushed to her bedroom. She had to write in her journal today. It had been a while since her last entry. However, this was one of the hardest days of her life.

Dear Journal,

Today my dad flew to Philadelphia to get Areebah. Areebah is the woman responsible for my mother's death. Although my father tried to convince me that she had nothing to do with Mom's death, I do not agree. Ever since we came back from Grandmom's funeral, mom was sad and she began drinking a lot.

Dad could have taken her to Alcoholics Anonymous or somewhere to get help. But, he just let her continue to drink. I don't see how he didn't see she was crying out for help the day she died. We had a "family" meeting and Mom was upset. This is how I found out about that Areebah lady. Before that, Mom was being mean to me. She was never mean before. But, when she blurted out why she was angry and drinking, I began to understand.

The worst part was when she grabbed her keys to go out. Although Dad tried to discourage her, he should have physically restrained her. I MISS MY MOMMY!!!!! Here I am the only girl in the house and no one understands anything I am going through. I used to talk to Mommy about everything. I WILL NOT LET AREEBAH TAKE THE PLACE OF MY MOM!!!

If she comes here to live, she's going to regret ever leaving Philadelphia. She's going to wish she never rekindled with my father. My goal in life is to make Areebah's life a living hell and for her to experience the pain my mother felt prior to her dying.

Jabari knocked on Salamah's door to see if she was ready to eat. As the door opened, Salamah jumped up startled and slammed the book shut. This movement piqued Jabari's interest.

"What are you writing?"

"Nothing!"

"Then why did you close the book so fast?"

"This is my journal and it's private."

"I know you're upset about Dad going up

there to meet Areebah; so am I. However, he has a right to be happy."

"I HATE her!" Salamah said as tears as big as raindrops began falling down her cheeks.

"Who, Areebah?"

"No, Mom!"

"Why?"

"She left us. She didn't have to jump in that car when she was so drunk. Why did she have to leave us?"

"I know Little Sis. I am still sad too."

"I want our family back. I don't want Dad to marry Areebah!"

"Salamah, I know that you're sad. It's been almost two years and Dad does deserve happiness in his life. Let's give Areebah a try."

"I'll give her something, alright!"

"Ever since Mom died Salamah, you've been very angry and made some poor decisions. I saved you from a lot of them and didn't tell Dad. Please don't do anything stupid. Areebah may have had a little to do with Mom's death, but it was Mom's decision to go out and drink and drive head on into a tractor trailer. We cannot blame Areebah for that."

"Okay, I won't."

Although Salamah told her brother that she wouldn't hold Areebah responsible for her mother's death; that was farthest from the truth. Salamah began to formulate her plan called "Operation Destroy Areebah". Salamah was certain that she would get in trouble if she executed her plan. However, she had to show her father how bad of an idea it was for him to bring Areebah into their house.

Thirty-One

Frankie arrived in Philadelphia; picked up his car; and headed to the hotel. Before going to see Areebah's dad, Frankie needed to rest. The flight was long and the time change had him with jet lag.

If I'm going to do this, I have to do this right. I cannot go to Brother Shafaat half-stepping.

After showering, Frankie turned on the television and lay down on the bed. Before he knew it he woke up and infomercials were on. He looked at his watch and realized he slept for eight hours. He decided to go back to sleep and the morning will begin the first day of the rest of his life.

"Ring! Ring! Ring!" The phone rang because Frankie needed to get up for the morning prayer, Fajr. He knew if he didn't call for a wakeup call, he would have overslept. Frankie got up and performed wudu. He then performed two Sunnah rakat and prayed Salatul Istikhara. He then performed Salatul Fajr.

After praying, Frankie entered the shower and lathered himself with a musk scented body wash. He then shampooed his hair and dried off. After dressing he went to visit Felicia.

Ding dong. Ding dong. Ding dong.

"Who is it?" Felicia shouted through the door.

Who is ringing my bell at this time in the morning? Felicia wondered.

Felicia peeped through the front window and was surprised at what she saw.

"Frankie! What are you doing here?"

"I came to Philly to take my little sister out to breakfast. Would you like to join me?"

"Sure, come in for a moment, let me get ready."

They drove to the restaurant and ate turkey bacon; eggs fried hard; and hash browned potatoes. He washed his breakfast with orange juice and water.

"I accepted Islam and I'm coming to ask Areebah to marry me."

"I knew it was just a matter of time. Why didn't you tell me you were coming? I would have set a room up for you."

"I wanted it to be a surprise. She doesn't know I'm in town."

"What?" Felicia popped her head up and stared at Frankie with her mouth open.

"Before I go see her, I'm going to talk to her father."

"YOU'RE going to talk to Brother Shafaat?"

"Yep!"

"What, do you have a death wish?

Frankie laughed at Felicia's statement. Everyone knew Shafaat hated Frankie. For Frankie to approach Shafaat about marrying Areebah was a significant step in their relationship.

"I guess you are serious about her. I can let you know that she is still interested in you. I just didn't tell you because I didn't know if you were still interested in her since you never mentioned her to me again."

"Really?" Frankie said as a smile spread across his face.

"Well, don't let her know that I am here. I don't want her to know yet. She doesn't even know I'm Muslim."

"You're going to make me cry. I always thought the two of you should be together. Don't get me wrong, I liked Laurie, but I always had a special place in my heart for Areebah."

"Me too! Well, I'm headed to talk to Brother Shafaat. I'll let you know what happened after I speak with him and Areebah."

"Okay, I love you Big Bro."

"I love you too."

Thirty-Two

"As salaamu alaikum Ummi, is Abi there?" Areebah said to her mother.

"Na'am, but he is still in a foul mood."

"I'm coming over; I've had enough of this nonsense. He has to stop brooding over this. When I come over, I want to speak with him alone."

"I think that's a great idea. I've been trying to get him out of this funk but to no avail. His anger confuses me."

Areebah hopped in her car and headed to her parents' house. She missed the banter between her and her father. She also wanted to know why he had such disdain for Frankie. While driving, Areebah practiced what she would say to him. As Areebah turned the corner onto her parents' block, she noticed the lawn was three inches overgrown as well as sprinkled with daffodils. On top of it all, a lot of litter was strewn about. Areebah walked in the yard shaking her head. She was more convinced than ever that she and her father had to talk.

"As salaamu alaikum!" Areebah said greeting the house as she let herself in.

"Wa laikum mus salaam. We're back here," Kashifah yelled from the back of the house.

Areebah walked into the back room and hugged her mom and then went to her dad.

"Abi, please don't go away I want to hug you. I also need to talk to you."

Kashifah walked out of the room to give Areebah and Shafaat time to talk.

"Abi, it's been well past the three day time frame for being angry. What's the real problem?"

"What are you talking about Areebah? I'm not angry with you."

"Ever since you walked in on Ummi and me talking about Frankie, you've been quite distant."

"Have I? I didn't realize it. I just felt that you and your mom wanted to talk so I always leave when you're here. I figure you two want to talk about Frankie again."

"That's what I'm talking about Abi, that sly remark was not necessary. What's the deal with you and Frankie anyway?"

A hush fell over the room. Shafaat began playing with a piece of paper near him. There was no eye contact between the two. This behavior aroused her interest even more.

"Abi, please look at me," she pleaded.

"Areebah, please come here and sit beside me."

She looked at her father and decided to walk towards him.

"What I'm going to tell you cannot be repeated to your mother."

More secrets? Areebah thought.

"Ok."

"During the sixties there was free love, free sex, and lack of responsibility. As you know, your mom, Inez, her husband, and I spent a lot of time together."

"Yes."

"Well, one time Inez and I partook in that free sex. We never discussed it with our spouses. However, not soon after, Inez was pregnant. I asked her often if Frankie was my son but she never responded."

All of a sudden Areebah felt like passing out. Heat rushed to her head and she felt dizzy. She held her head down and asked so low that Shafaat had to strain to hear her, "Why didn't you take a DNA test?"

"I wanted to but Inez refused. She wouldn't even talk to me about the situation."

"Now I understand your anger towards us being together. But, Inez has been dead for two and a half years, why didn't you reach out to Frankie since then?"

"What was I supposed to say? 'Frankie, I may be your father. Let's go take a test.'"

"That would have been a start. And since you knew that we liked each other, why didn't you tell me when I was younger?"

"Many times I was tempted, however, when I saw that the two of you went in different directions and subsequently got married, I thought the situation remained in the past."

She recollected the times the families got together. Her father was never in the company of Inez. She always attributed it to them being Muslim; however, after hearing this information, all the pieces fell into place.

"So, when I entered the house and overheard you and your mother discussing Frankie, I was angry that you two excluded me from the conversation; and frightened that after nearly fifty years, the truth may have to come out. I figured if I sulked and behaved poorly towards you, you would change your mind."

"Well Abi, Frankie and I are getting serious and I intend on marrying him. Therefore, if you think there is any chance of him being my brother, please let him know so you two can be tested."

"But why would you want to marry a kaffir?"

"Abi, that brings me to the other reason I'm here. Instead of talking to me, you call my children and tell them I'm interested in a kaffir. Why would you do that?"

"I didn't have anyone else to talk to regarding your situation. I know you raised your children in Islam so I figured if they talked to you maybe they could change your mind."

"Abi, at this time, no one can change my mind. My children are living their lives. You and Ummi have your lives; and I'm alone."

"But there are so many brothers out there interested in marrying you."

"I know that Abi. But, I'm not interested in them. I don't want to marry someone and Frankie becomes available and I can't marry him."

"Areebah, I didn't know that your feelings for him are that strong. I'll contact him. Can you get me his number?"

"Na'am. Let me get his information from the car. I left my phone in the car because I wanted to be sure that we weren't disturbed during this conversation."

"Areebah, you know I love you and I want the best for you."

"I know Abi, that's why when you stopped talking to me I was sad."

"I'm sorry Sweetie. I never meant to hurt you. Everything I did was to protect you."

Or protect yourself, Areebah thought.

"Okay Abi, I'll be right back. I'm going to the car to get the number."

Areebah walked into the living room and her mother gave Areebah a puzzled look.

"What happened in there?"

"Abi and I had a serious talk. I have to get some information for him out of the car."

Thirty-Three

Frankie rehearsed his speech as he headed to Shafaat's house.

"As salaamu alaikum Brother Shafaat. How are you? I've taken my Shahadah and I'm here to ask your permission to marry Areebah. She doesn't know I'm here and I wanted to come to you as one Muslim man to another. Now, whether you give permission or not, I'm still going to ask her to be my wife. I just wanted to be courteous and ask you first. I know that you never liked me and you never wanted the two of us to be together; but, I think the Qadr of Allah subhana wa ta'ala is for us to be together. Therefore, I hope I have your support."

Sweat poured down Frankie's face. His hands were trembling and he could no longer concentrate. Why would a man of 49 years of age with children and grandchildren and be afraid to talk to another man. Maybe it's not fear, just the sense of the unknown. Being so occupied with his rehearsed speech and thoughts, Frankie pulled in front of the Abdul Matin residence quicker than he expected.

"Well, here goes nothing," he said out loud to no one in particular.

Frankie walked towards the front door still practicing his speech to Shafaat. Just as he was about to knock on the door, the door swung wide open.

"Frankie?"

"Areebah?"

They both stared at each other as if each saw a ghost.

"Is Frankie really here? Am I hallucinating?" Areebah said pinching herself.

"Why are you pinching yourself? I'm really here." Frankie said laughing.

"Is that a kufi I see on your head and a beard?"

"Yep," Frankie said not offering any additional information.

"Why are you here at my parents' house?" Areebah said still trying to wrap her head around why Frankie was standing in front of her.

"I've taken my Shahadah and I am here to ask your father's permission to marry you."

"Areebah!" Frankie said catching her before she hit the ground.

Just then, Kashifah and Shafaat walked to the door to see what all the commotion was. Both stood at the door dumbfounded for a few seconds and then they realize that Areebah fainted and was leaning in Frankie's arms.

"Bring her inside," Kashifah said fanning her daughter trying to get her to awaken.

"What are you doing here Frankie?" Shafaat asked moving back and forth from the front door to the kitchen.

"I came to tell you that I accepted Islam as my Deen (way of life) and am asking your permission to marry Areebah."

"Alhamdulillah," Kashifah said.

"Frankie, please come with me to the back of the house."

"Areebah, Honey, wake up."

"Ummi, I think I'm seeing things. I opened the door and Frankie was standing at the front door."

"You're not seeing things, Areebah. Frankie is here. He's in the back now talking to your dad about marrying you. He told us he took his Shahadah."

She closed her eyes and tears ran down her face.

"Areebah baby, why are you crying?"

"I can't believe that he's here. These are tears of joy," Areebah lied to her mother.

Is Abi telling Frankie that he thinks he's his father?

"Frankie, I brought you back here because

Areebah and I were just talking about you."

"Really? What were you talking about?"

"I was telling her the history of your parents, Kashifah, and myself."

"Wasn't it great how close our families were? Now we can be really family now, Alhamdulillah."

"I need you to sit down for a moment. What I'm about to tell you is hard for me. But, I must tell you."

Frankie noticed Shafaat pacing back and forth and wrenching his hands. Is he about to tell me that he doesn't want Areebah and me to get married? Me coming here is just a formality. I don't want to disrespect her father; however, this is something that we both want and he will not get between the two of us again.

"Frankie," Shafaat began not knowing where to start.

"When we were much younger, your mother and I had relations. Nine or so months later you were born. I asked your mom if you were my son but she would never answer my question."

"Oh that."

"Oh that? What does that mean?"

"My mother told me that a long time ago. My father and I had a paternity test and the results were 99.999% that he was my father."

"Alhamdulillah," Shafaat said with almost fifty years of guilt rushing from his shoulders. He felt lighter than he did earlier that day.

"Well, back to what you said in the other room. I would love for you to marry my daughter."

"Brother Shafaat, may I ask you a question that's bothered me for the past four months?"

"Yes, what's that question?"

"Why didn't you ever invite me to the Deen of Al-Islam?"

"As I said earlier, I thought it was a possibility that I was your father and I felt that by not teaching you about the Deen that you and Areebah will never get together."

"So in essence, you're telling me that because of your indiscretions and secrets that you kept me from living my life as a Muslim? May Allah subhana wa ta'ala have mercy on your soul and forgive your sins."

"Ameen. Yes, it was selfish of me and there is no way I can make it up to you. I just told Areebah about my concerns with you. That may be one of the reasons she passed out when she saw you. She was going to the car to get your phone number so I could call you."

"Well, we need to go right out there and tell her not to worry and that we can get married."

"Wait a minute! I haven't told Kashifah. Bring Areebah back here and tell her."

"Don't you think over fifty years of secrets are enough?"

"I guess," Shafaat said rubbing his forehead.

Just then Areebah and Kashifah walked into

the room.

"You guess what?" Kashifah said.

The three of them looked at one another. Shafaat stepped forward.

"Kashifah, I need to talk to you. Please have a seat."

The stillness of the air alerted Kashifah that something was wrong. Shafaat talked on and on while Frankie refused to look up from his phone. He behaved as if he were expecting someone to call him at any time.

"What's…going…on?" Kashifah said with caution. "Since you and Areebah had your father-daughter conversation, you too have been more secretive than usual. Then Frankie arrives and Areebah faints. Who is going to tell me what is happening here?"

"First I want to tell you that I love you. I cannot imagine how my life would have been had we not married."

Out the corner of her eye, Kashifah noticed Frankie trying to move as far away from her as possible, while Areebah was between crying and murmuring to herself.

"I love you too. But what does that have to do with whatever is happening here?"

"Do you remember back when we were in the Struggle?"

"Yeeesss."

"Remember all the fun we had back then. The most important thing was the uplifting of our people."

"Yea, I remember all of that. But I do not understand why you're bringing all of that up now."

"One time Inez and I drink a little too much and we ended up together."

"What do you mean ended up together?" Kashifah demanded.

"We had sexual relations. It was only one time and after that time I made sure never to be in her presence again."

"Again, I don't understand why that is important now," Kashifah said getting an instant headache.

All of a sudden, everyone stopped moving and the room was as silent as the masjid during Zuhr prayer. Looking from Shafaat to Areebah and then to Frankie, it seemed as if the fog was lifted. Kashifah remembered Inez mentioning it to her after it happened decades ago. She never brought it up to Shafaat. So she wondered why he was telling her this now.

"Shafaat, we were all young and adventurous then. But what I don't know is why you are bringing this to me now."

"I thought Frankie was my son."

Thirty-Four

"Dad called," Jabari told his siblings.

"Is he on his way home?" Chabata said.

"Not yet, he said he has some important news to share with us."

"He better not tell me he married that bitch Areebah!"

"Salamah, you've got to calm down. Mom's been gone for almost two years. Areebah did not bother us or our father all that time. Don't you think he has the right to be happy?"

"You may be right Jabari, but I still don't like it and no one can make me."

"Alright Salamah," Jabari said giving in to his sister.

"I'm going upstairs. I need to prepare for Dad when he arrives."

"I didn't even tell you when he arrives."

"It doesn't matter. I have a lot of planning and I want everything to be just right when he arrives."

Salamah planned to discourage her dad from marrying Areebah. If he insisted on marrying Areebah, they will have to deal with her wrath.

After Salamah stomped up the stairs and slammed her room door, Jabari called Frankie.

"Dad, I don't think Salamah is in a good place right now."

"What makes you say that son?"

"Right after you left to go to Philly; she was up writing in her diary. When I asked her what she's doing, she snapped at me and became defensive."

"Well Jabari, she's still having a difficult time dealing with the death of your mother. If I wasn't in such a funk, maybe I would have recognized it sooner. She's just grieving."

"Dad, this is a little more than grieving. A couple of months after Mom died, while you were deep in your depression, Salamah was suspended for fighting. She banged a girl's head so hard and so many times on the floor that the paramedics were called."

"Why didn't anyone tell me of this," Frankie said angry and disappointed in himself for letting his baby girl experience these events alone.

"That's just one incident I was able to talk to the principal and inform them that our mother died and our father is in a deep depression. Only because of those circumstances was she not suspended or even expelled."

"What was the other incident?" Frankie said afraid to hear anymore.

"One day I told her to cook dinner because she hasn't been helping around the house. She cooked and added rat poison to the food. Rat poison Dad! I caught it before she served the food. But, I think she needs to enter counseling quickly. I think she wants to hurt Areebah if you decide to marry her."

"Why would she hurt Areebah?" Frankie figured it had something to do with Laurie's death.

"She still blames Areebah for Mom killing herself. I tried numerous times to let her know that Mom decided on her own to drive drunk. But in her eyes, the blame lies all on Areebah."

"Okay, I've heard enough. Please let me speak with my daughter."

Jabari called for Salamah. She didn't respond. He called a little louder with more authority, still no response.

"Son, walk up to her room and hand her the phone."

Walking up the steps in slow motion, Jabari went to Salamah's room and tapped on the door. He did not like being in her presence because each day her behavior became darker and darker. After a little jousting back and forth, Salamah answered the phone.

"Hello."

"Hey Baby Girl, how are you?"

"Good."

"What's up with the monosyllabic responses?"

"I'm busy and Jabari is always picking with me."

"You're too busy to talk to your dad?"

"No, sorry Dad."

"Apology accepted. What's this I hear about you still blaming Areebah for the death of your mom?"

"Dad, while she did not give Mom the drink and the keys, her presence is what drove Mom to drink and kill herself."

"Salamah, I understand your logic. However, it is flawed. What your mother did falls directly into her lap. Please Salamah. I love you. Please don't do anything to hurt Areebah or me."

"I won't do anything to hurt you."

Thirty-Five

"Your son?"

"Yes."

"Why didn't you tell me?"

"Well...uh…um…"

"What's all the stammering about?"

Kashifah wanted Shafaat to continue to sweat. She and Inez discussed this decades ago. She'd been waiting for her husband to tell her and he never did. Why did it take for Frankie to come and ask to marry Areebah for him to tell her? Kashifah stood in the doorway with her hands on her hips and her eyes piercing at Shafaat waiting for his response.

"I knew how close you and Inez were and I didn't want to get between the two of you."

"But Shafaat, you did. We stopped

communicating because every time the families got together you would either become distant or find a way to excuse yourself."

"When it first happened we were not in a good place. Once everything settled, you and I were doing well and I didn't want to upset the applecart."

"So you looked at me as an applecart?"

Kashifah always wondered why Shafaat never mentioned that he thought Frankie was his son so she pushed for more information. She didn't care if he had to sit there and sweat and find the words, everything had to be unveiled today.

"No, I never looked at you as an applecart. However, we were growing well as a family and then you became pregnant with Areebah. It was the happiest moment in my life and since Inez never pushed the issue, I swept it to the back of my mind."

"But did you really sweep it to the back of your mind Shafaat?"

"Yes, I did."

"I don't think so."

"Why do you say that?"

"Because if you did, you would not have avoided Frankie as he and Areebah were growing up. And you definitely would not have gotten so angry when Areebah and I were discussing him a few months ago."

"Kashifah," Shafaat eyes moistened as he wrung his hands, "I never wanted to hurt you and

I didn't want Areebah to get hurt. When I saw that they grew apart and both got married, I felt the issue resolved itself."

"But Shafaat, we all know that what happens in the dark always comes to the light."

"Haqq (truth). But, now that Frankie and I talked, Inez told him years ago and he and his father had a DNA test and, 'I am NOT the father.'" Shafaat said trying to interject some humor into the situation.

"I know you are not the father. Inez and I discussed this back when they were little children."

"So you let me go through all of this and you knew he wasn't my son?" Shafaat said shaking his head as he looked at his wife.

"You let me go almost fifty years and never talked to me about it, so what are a few minutes."

Silence swept through the room. Frankie and Areebah looked at each other and then looked at Shafaat and Kashifah. The tension was so thick in the room that a finely sharpened knife could make slices as thin as a delicatessen worker does when slicing cold cuts.

"Well, I guess we have a wedding to plan!" Kashifah said with enthusiasm diminishing the tension.

"I guess we do," Shafaat said with apprehension.

Areebah and Frankie looked into each other's eyes and both saw happiness that they haven't had in years. She was ready to cry; jump into Frankie's arms; and kiss him all at once. However, she knew that was not proper behavior for a Muslim woman to portray. After a brief silence, Frankie spoke.

"Well Brother Shafaat, I came here with a prepared speech but as we all know, Allah is the best of planners."

"Ameen!" They said in unison.

"I haven't spoken with Areebah in a while and I didn't let her know about me accepting my Shahadah or coming here to ask her to marry me. If possible, may I please have a few minutes with her?" Frankie said looking back and forth between Kashifah and Shafaat.

"Na'am, please let me not stand in your way any longer."

"Allah always answers du'a," Kashifah whispered in Areebah's ears as she hugged her before they left the room.

"Frankie, I'm so happy you're here. Why didn't you tell me you took your Shahadah?"

"After learning more and more about Al-Islam, I realized that I wanted to do everything correctly and I didn't want to continue communicating with you because I know it could have moved from the doubtful to haram."

"At least you could have told me you were coming to Philly. I could have prepared for you."

"Since I knew your dad never wanted us to get married, I wanted to speak with him first. I know you told me that you didn't care what anyone said. However, as I studied Islam more and more, I know that no marriage is valid without a Wakil and a contract."

"True. I've made istikhara and strong du'a. I always trusted and believed in Allah. He always answered my du'a."

While Areebah was talking, Frankie admired her beauty. He loved how she grew into a voluptuous woman. Although she had on a jilbab (long dress) and khimar (head covering), he could still see her curves. He was happy with the decision he made. He was apprehensive before he showed up; but now it was clear that the trip was worth it.

"Why are you looking at me like that?"

"I never thought you could get any more beautiful. However, you are both beautiful and sexy."

"Now how in the world can you tell that I'm sexy?"

"Don't worry about that, just know that you are."

"How do your children feel about us getting married?"

"Well, Yobachi and Chata are ecstatic. Jabari understands why I decided to marry you. Salamah, well, we have some work with her."

"Really?"

"Yeah, she's having a tough time. When I was going through my depression, I didn't know that she was also experiencing the same feelings. Jabari just told me that she's done some things that he didn't bother me with. At this time she is not receptive to us getting married."

"Then do you think we should get married?"

"Absolutely! Before I came down here, I told my children that regardless of their feelings, I'm getting married because I deserve happiness."

"Maa shaa Allah. You're about to have me cry again."

"No need to cry. I don't ever want to be the cause of your tears. We took all of this time to be together. In shaa Allah, we'll spend the remainder of our lives loving each other."

"I'm looking forward to it. Ever since that day at the café, I've dreamed of this."

"What about your children? How do they feel about you getting married?"

"Well, Sahlah is kind of upset with me because all of her life I've told her to marry a Muslim man and not to 'convert a brother'. So she feels as if I am being hypocritical."

"Convert a brother, huh?" Frankie said laughing. "I've never heard that before."

"Well, many times Muslim sisters get fed up with the shenanigans of the brothers that they make the joke that they will 'convert a brother'."

"Boy, the things I have to learn about the Islamic culture."

"I wouldn't necessarily call it the Islamic culture. However, I would call it part of the

African-American experience within Islam."

"You always had a way with words. Every time we talk, you give me more and more reasons why I love you. What about your son? What does he think?"

"He said if I'm happy he's happy. However, my son is into himself so if it doesn't negatively affect him he doesn't worry about it."

"Well, it seems like it's those daughters we have to work on."

They both laughed at this. However, Frankie's laugh was a little more nervous than Areebah's. He didn't know how Salamah was going to react when he let them know that the wedding will go on.

"What about living arrangements? Are you ready to pick up and move already?"

"I didn't even think that far. Honestly, although I believed that you would become Muslim and you and I would get married, I didn't think I would be surprised with the announcement."

"Well, I remember what you always told me when we were growing up. When we reconnected, not once but twice, I decided to learn more about Al-Islam. After learning about it and deciding to make it my way of life, I knew that you and I would get married."

"Frankie, I want to marry you. However, I never thought about moving to San Diego."

Each time Frankie looked at Areebah and

heard her speak he fell deeper in love. By no chance will he let geography be an obstacle for them again.

"Listen Areebah," he said with earnest.

She turned towards him to hear what he had to say.

"For decades you and I were separated by geography and family. Although neither of us thought about the other, which is now in the past. I will neither allow family nor geography to be obstacles for us ever again, in shaa Allah."

"Go on," she said with a smile so wide that it made Frankie chuckle just a bit.

"I know we have issues we need to address with our respective daughters. I also know that I came to you from left field so I don't expect you to move right away, or at all. The only thing I do want is to marry you before I go back home. I know we haven't discussed a dowry, but I'm financially able to give you whatever you ask and I'm willing to provide it for you at this moment. If I'm rushing you, please let me know and I will go home and wait for you. The ball is now in your court."

Areebah was taken aback by his forwardness. But more than that, she was surprised at how he laid the cards on the table.

"First, I love you so much and I definitely want to marry you. But, first, let me speak with my parents. When are you scheduled to leave?"

"I have an open ticket. I'll go to the hotel. You

have my number. Call me as soon as you and your parents are done talking. "

After walking Frankie to the door, Areebah called her parents. As she turned around, they were both smiling like the Cheshire Cat.

"Did you hear his proposal?"

"Yes. Are you hesitant about marrying him now?" Kashifah said concerned.

"No, not at all; however, although I know that I consistently say I am able to make my own decisions, I've always trusted the advice from the two of you. What do you think?"

"I think you should follow your heart," said Kashifah.

"There's no reason in prolonging it. I've kept the two of you apart long enough. He appears to be genuine. You have my support and blessing."

"Alhamdulillah! I love you Ummi and Abi!"

"We love you too," they said as they embraced one another.

"I'm going to give him a little time to rest at the hotel. I'm going to go home and freshen up. I'll call a few friends over and we can do the nikah (marriage ceremony) tonight. Is it okay to do it here?"

"Absolutely!" Kashifah said without checking with Shafaat.

"Of course Sweetheart, you are our only child; where else would we have you get married?" Shafaat said making sure his daughter knew that she had his full support.

Thirty-Six

Areebah headed home and called a few friends. She called Baqir and then Sahlah to let them know that she's getting married in a couple of hours.

"Aww Ummi, that's great! In shaa Allah you'll be as happy with him as you were with Abi," Baqir stated.

"What kind of dowry is he giving you? Is it money?"

"Baqir, why must you always ask about money when you speak with me? Anyway, whatever the dowry is, it's mine. Go get a job!"

"I just want to make sure you'll be well taken care of."

"Okay Son, whatever you say. I have to call your sister now. As salaamu alaikum. I love you."

"Wa laikum mus salaam, I love you too. But seriously Ummi before you hang up, do you have one hundred dollars I can borrow until the first?"

"Bye Boy!"

Now the difficult conversation, Areebah thought.

"As salaamu alaikum Sahlah."

"Wa laikum mus salaam Ummi. How are you?"

"I'm well, Alhamdulillah. You'll never guess who showed up at your grandparent's house?"

"I'm not good at guessing Ummi. Who showed up?"

"Frankie."

"Who?"

"Frankie."

"Who is Frankie?"

"The man I told you about that I knew when I was growing up."

"And why are you telling me that he showed up to their house?"

"He's asked me to marry him."

"So you're telling me that you're going to marry a kafir? All these years you lecture me about marrying a Muslim and you are going against your own words."

"Who said I was marrying a kafir?"

"You did."

"No, I said I was marrying Frankie."

"Last I heard he was a kafir."

"As I told you previously, he's not a kafir, he was just in the state of jahaliyah."

"Whatever, either way he's not a Muslim."

"That's what I wanted to tell you before you jumped down my throat. He came to your grandparents to tell your grandfather that he accepted Al-Islam and he wants to marry me."

"SubhanAllah."

"In shaa Allah, we'll be getting married in a couple of hours."

"What's the rush?"

"Well, neither of us is getting younger. Also, this was a long time in waiting."

"But Ummi, what do you really know about him?"

"Sahlah, what do we really know about anyone before we get married?"

"I just think you're rushing. Shouldn't you wait a little longer?"

"Wait. What am I waiting for?"

"Don't you miss Abi?"

"Of course I do but what does that have to do with anything?"

"I think it's too soon."

"Sahlah, I called you just to let you know. Honestly, it's not about what you think. And also, you know as well as I that the iddah for a widow is four months and ten days. It's been well over three years since your father died. No amount of waiting will ever bring him back to this world."

"It's your life Ummi You're going to do what you want anyway."

"You're absolutely right Sahlah. I just wanted to tell you about my good news and I do not feel good vibes from you."

"Ummi, it's just that for all of these years I wanted to get married. I told you about different men who were interested in me who were not Muslim and you discouraged me from interacting with them. Then you do the exact opposite of how you counseled me. So, I am not happy for you."

"I understand your feelings Sahlah. However, you're reading into this incorrectly and each time I bring up the conversation, you do not allow me enough time to explain how everything happened."

"That's just it Ummi; I don't want you to explain anything to me. I have to go now. It's time for me to get ready for work. As salaamu alaikum."

"Wa laikum mus salaam. I love you Sahlah."

"I love you too Ummi."

Areebah disconnected the phone and promised herself that she would not let Sahlah's sour mood spoil her night. She found her favorite fragrance and body wash that has vanilla and coconut in it. She then pulled out a black long satin slip to put on under her raspberry chiffon butterfly jilbab embroidered with rhinestones on the collar and sleeves. She coupled it with a dark pink hijab trimmed in rhinestones. She completed her wardrobe with a pair of Nine West silver fabric camya. She decided to call Frankie and let him know there was going to be a wedding.

Thirty-Seven

Frankie drove back to the hotel on cloud nine. He didn't remember making any of the turns. All of a sudden he found himself in front of the parking gate. He couldn't wait to get into the room. He wanted to prepare the room for a special night for him and Areebah if she called him tonight to get married. He also needed to call his children to let them know what's happening.

Before setting the room up and preparing himself, Frankie decided to call his children. He was not looking forward to the conversation with Salamah. However, this conversation had to occur and he was not going to let anyone put a damper on his night. He decided to speak with the boys first in order to have a little of excitement before the discussion with Salamah.

"Hello."

"Hello Jabari, this is Dad."

"Hey Dad," Jabari said happy to hear his dad's voice. "How's everything there?"

"Things are great!"

"Really?"

"Really!"

"Do tell."

"Well, the day started out great. I went to see your aunt and we talked and went out to eat. It was great meeting with her and reminiscing."

"Dad, you know I don't want to know about what you and Aunt Felicia talked about."

"Okay Son, you're right. After leaving your Aunt Felicia – see I told you that part was important – I drove to Areebah's parent's house. Before seeing her I wanted to give the respect to her father. When I pulled up into the driveway, I was rehearsing what I was going to say to him and was not paying attention to my surroundings. While still rehearsing my speech, I rang the doorbell. The door opened just as I pushed the bell and Areebah was standing right at the door!"

"No!"

"Yep, she actually passed out."

"She passed out? Why?"

"She and her father were just talking about me. He was telling her that he thought he was my father."

"What? Hold up Dad. What are you talking about him being your father?"

"That's not the important part."

"That's not the important part. Are you about to marry your sister?"

"Boy! Are you nuts? No I'm not going to marry my sister. Okay, since you insist, I'll make a long story short. Before I was born – of course – my mother and Areebah's father had a little fling. My mother became pregnant a little time after that and all these years he thought he was my father. I always knew he wasn't because Mom told me a long time ago about the situation and my dad and I had a DNA test. Now, may I get back to the part of the story I want to tell?"

"Okay Dad, go ahead. I just wanted to make sure we weren't getting into any incest here."

"No, no incest here. Anyway, I told them that I took my Shahadah and I want to marry Areebah. After clearing the air of the history of the two families, Areebah's mother and father gave me their blessing. I told Areebah I want to marry her tonight and she wanted some time to talk to her parents. So I came back to the hotel so they could have time to talk privately."

"What if she doesn't call back? What if she tells you she doesn't want to marry you?"

"Son, I'm pretty good at reading women, especially women I love. She'll be calling me back. We haven't made decisions regarding where she's going to live. However, the plan is to get married tonight."

"That sounded like an intense time. I wish I were there. When are you coming home?"

"I'm not sure. Why? Is everything okay?"

"Well…yeah."

"What's going on Jabari? Is it Salamah again?"

"Yes. I didn't want to bother you with this. But I think the longer you are away the angrier she's becoming. I think she may hurt herself or someone else."

"What is she doing?"

"She snaps on everyone. She's constantly up in her room. She walks around with a scowl on her face. I just don't know how to talk to her anymore."

"I can't promise that I'll rush back. But I will be back as soon as possible. Where are Chata and Yobachi?"

"They're outside playing. Would you like me to get them?"

"No, that's alright. What about Salamah? Where is she?"

"She's in her room; one moment."

While Frankie waited for his youngest daughter to come to the phone he thought about the treatment center he went to when he was depressed. When he gets back to town, he's going to take Salamah before she reached the point of no return.

"Hey Daddy," Salamah greeted her father trying to sound upbeat.

"Hey Baby Girl, how are you?"

"I'm doing fine. How are you?" She said with her standard response.

"I want to give you some news and I want you to be happy for me."

"You're marrying HER."

"Yes, I will be marrying Areebah; more than likely tonight."

"Tonight?"

"Yes."

"Why so soon?"

"So soon? Salamah, you know I came up here with the sole purpose of marrying her."

"I thought you two would have had at least a year engagement."

"Remember before I left I reminded you all that I became a Muslim and I want to do things correctly. Well, one of those things is marrying Areebah and not just talking or whatever."

"Are you bringing her home when you come?"

"Probably not."

"Good. I hope she never comes down here."

"She's a good woman. I think when you meet her you will really get to like her."

"I don't need another mother."

"Did anyone say anything about making her another mother?"

"Isn't that how it goes?"

"Listen Salamah, I know you're not happy about this. However, when I was home I told you that I did not want to spend the remainder of my life alone and that Areebah is the person I want to spend the remainder of my life with."

Beep. Beep.

"Is that her calling you now?"

"Yes it is. Let me call you back."

"See, you already are putting her before me."

"That's unfair Salamah. I'll talk to you later. I love you."

Salamah disconnected the phone without responding to Frankie. He decided that it was important to get Salamah into therapy. He just hoped he didn't wait too long and that irreparable damage occurred.

Ring. Ring.

Frankie forgot about the other line.

"As salaamu alaikum."

"Wa laikum mus salaam," Areebah said with the sultriest voice Frankie ever heard from her.

"So, what's the verdict?" Frankie held his breath waiting for the reply. Although he told Jabari he could read women, it's been so long since Laurie that he second guessed himself.

"Are you available in an hour?"

"Just tell me when and where and I'll be there ten minutes early."

"Okay, meet me at my parents' house. You may want to dress a little more formal. We's gon' git married!"

They both laughed.

"I have to start getting ready. I'll see you in about an hour in shaa Allah. As salaamu alaikum future zawj."

"Wa laikum mus salaam. What is a zawj?"

"Zawj is husband in Arabic."

"Ooohhh. How do you say wife?"

"Zawjati."

"Then you should be my zawjati in less than two hours, in shaa Allah."

Frankie and Areebah disconnected their phones and began to prepare for the nikah.

Frankie decorated the room and put on some soft music. He heard that many Muslims do not like listening to music; he hoped that Areebah liked listening to music and appreciated the selection he chose. He then took out the sparkling cider and the champagne flutes. After placing the sparkling cider in the ice bucket, he lit some incense to add aroma to the room. He couldn't believe it, in shaa Allah, he and Areebah will be together after all this time. He prayed that there will be no problems. Frankie began thinking about the mini vacations he planned with Laurie and each time something catastrophic occurred. He prayed to Allah that this time nothing catastrophic happened.

Thirty-Eight

Areebah on the other hand was on cloud nine. She took her time to bathe and enjoy the aroma coming from the tub as well as the aroma from the candles she lit. After bathing, she applied lotion to her entire body and then put on the black satin slip. She wrapped her hair while she bathed. After getting out of the bath, she combed it out to make sure when she unwrapped herself for her husband that the gift looked better than the wrapping.

After verifying that her hair will be smooth, she rewrapped it. She then commenced to get dress and put on her chiffon dress and hijab. She put a little lipstick on and kohl around her eyes. The piece de resistance, she put on her shoes.

In shaa Allah, Frankie will love what he sees when he walks into my parents' house. Areebah thought to herself.

He'll have the surprise of a lifetime when they go back to the hotel. She couldn't wait until she could take a ghusl (a purification shower) for other than Jumuah or because it's the end of her menstrual cycle.

Areebah headed over to her parents' house where a couple of her friends should be there waiting for her. As she arrived and went inside, her breath was taken away. Her mother outdid herself. The backyard was decorated with various flowers such as lilies, roses, and daisies. There were balloons and chairs decorated with her favorite colors black and red. What really surprised her was the amount of guests. There were at least thirty guests and they all looked beautiful. Tears welled up in her eyes.

Frankie arrived ten minutes after Areebah. This time he paid more attention to his surroundings. There were more cars than usual in the neighborhood. *I know Areebah said she invited a couple of friends. I wonder how many people are here.* He asked himself. Frankie opened the door and was greeted by Shafaat.

"As salaamu alaikum Frankie."

"Wa laikum mus salaam. You look nice."

"Maa shaa Allah. It isn't everyday my baby girl gets married."

Frankie was smiling ear-to-ear. As they walked towards the back of the house he heard the murmur of many voices. It sounded much more than a couple. He exited into the back yard and was in awe of the view. He was even more impressed with the amount of people in attendance and how well dressed they were. Shafaat took Frankie to the seat where he and Areebah would sit and Frankie sat down with butterflies in his stomach.

Three minutes later Frankie heard Ein Klein Nachtmusik by Mozart and looked up. When he looked up, he saw the most beautiful site he'd seen in years. Areebah seemed to float down the aisle. Her face sparkled and the dress flowed. He thought how blessed he was to marry this woman. She walked in his direction and took a seat. Frankie was nervous because he never attended an Islamic wedding and he didn't know what to expect. She sat beside Frankie as the imam walked in front of the attendees and explained how a Muslim wedding was performed.

"One of the most important aspects of an Islamic wedding is the contract. No marriage is valid without a contract," he began.

"Also, the bride and groom must decide on a mahr, which is a dowry. Unlike the dowry many heard of, this mahr is a gift to the wife from her husband. It is also necessary for the woman to have a Wakil which is a guardian. In this case, the guardian is the bride's father."

The imam proceeded to perform the nikah, wedding ceremony, and within a few minutes Frankie and Areebah were married.

"I can't believe it, we're finally married,"

Areebah said as she and Frankie entered the hotel room.

"I am glad to have you Mrs. Williams."

"Hold up! Mrs. Williams?"

"Yes, now that we are married, aren't you taking my last name?"

"No. I didn't take my first husband's name and I am not taking your name either. Islamically, a woman doesn't have to take her husband's name."

"I don't understand what the big deal is; why not just take my name?"

"Since I'm my father's only child, I promised that I would always keep his last name."

"We'll shelve this conversation to later. I don't want to ruin our first night as a married couple."

Shelve this conversation. Obviously he doesn't realize the importance of me keeping my last name. When it comes back up, I'll explain it to without too much emotion.

She looked around the room and was impressed. In the bathroom was a heart-shaped whirlpool. As she walked in, the lighting was low with candles flickering. The music playing in the background was smooth and not overbearing. When she faced the bed, she was surprised when she saw a very sexy corset and v-string panty set lying on the bed.

Areebah was nervous. One would think this was her first marriage. Although she and Murad have been married for more than twenty years, she'd not been with another man. Shades of red appeared on her face. When she turned around, Frankie was smiling at her and she melted.

"Try it on."

"It's beautiful Frankie. How did you know my size?"

"When I love someone, I pay attention to everything. Every time you and I got together I looked at you and imagined what you would look like in sexy lingerie. I then went to the store and described you to the sales person."

"SubhanAllah! Really?" Areebah began feeling more self-conscious. As with many women, she was not comfortable in her skin. She felt she could lose weight in her stomach and hips. However, after seeing the loving looks from Frankie, she began to get comfortable.

"If you don't want to change into this right away, it's fine. I know this must be difficult for you. We can definitely take the time to really get to know each other. I want our marriage to last the rest of our lifetime so I want you to be ready to take me wholly as your husband."

Overcome with intense love for Frankie, Areebah didn't think she could love him anymore. Just then, he walked behind her and grabbed her waist. It's been so long since she's felt the firm, warm touch of a man that she just melted in his hands.

Allahu Akbar, Allahu Akbar! Allahu Akbar, Allahu Akbar! Ash hadu illaha il Allah!!...

"Well Baby, it's time to pray," Frankie said to Areebah.

"Alhamdulillah, our first prayer as husband and wife. In shaa Allah, we'll have so many more prayers together," Areebah said smiling from ear to ear.

She entered the bathroom to perform wudu. She stared in the mirror for a while.

"Allahumma anta has anta khalqi fahssin khuluqi (O Allah, just as you have made my external features beautiful, make my character beautiful as well.)" She prayed while looking at herself. After performing wudu, she exited the bathroom so Frankie could prepare for salah.

"Next time we'll take a ghusl," she said to him oozing sensuality as she brushed past him. She was looking forward to this new chapter in her life.

Frankie returned from the bathroom and they performed Salatul Maghrib (sunset prayer); since he was travelling, he combined his prayers and performed Salatul 'Isha (night prayer) as well. Areebah was surprised to hear Frankie recite some of the surahs from the Qur'an. She was apprehensive about him leading her in prayer because she'd heard horror stories of husbands who recited Surah Al-Fatiha so wrong that the wives prayed in secret again for fear of their prayers not being answered.

"Not bad for a rookie," Frankie turned around and said after he prayed as if he read

Areebah's mind. All she could do was laugh.

"Naw, not too bad at all; now, let's see what else you have that's good," she said in a seductive voice.

"Well, I bought some food and drinks, I think they're pretty good too," he said pretending as if he didn't catch the sexual innuendo.

"Food's nice, I'm sure we'll need it to recharge our batteries very soon. I'll be right back."

She disappeared in the restroom after picking up the lingerie from the bed and getting her cosmetic bag out of the closet. Tomorrow I'll encourage him to join me in the hot tub. She filled the tub with a wood fragranced bath and shower gel. She stepped her right foot into the tub testing the temperature. She loved to take hot baths. The water was cool enough for her to settle into the tub.

For a brief moment, sadness rushed over her. Thoughts of Murad rushed through her. Although she was ready and it was halal for her to remarry, a twinge of guilt went through her soul. She lay back in the tub for a while reliving the past three years. She thought how no one could have told her five years ago that Murad would be gone and she would be married to Frankie!

Having languished in the tub long enough, she bathed herself and rinsed all of the suds off of her caramel skin. She then took out the body butter with the same fragrance of the bath cream and made sure to moisturize every part of her body.

She wanted her husband to see the beautiful brown skin she had sans ash. She also used powder to dust herself.

"Areebah, Baby? Are you okay in there?" Frankie said waiting with abated breath for his wife to be with him.

"Yes My Love. I'm on my way out."

Frankie was looking at television because he thought she would be in the bathroom a little longer.

"As salaamu alaikum zawji," Areebah said with as much sensuality and seduction she could muster.

Frankie turned around and the remote and his mouth dropped at the same time. Frozen in place for a few seconds, Frankie got up and moved closer to his wife.

"Not yet Baby, please go freshen yourself up first."

Frankie unzipped his pants and let them fall to the floor. He rushed to take off his shirt and threw it where the pants were. He rushed into the bathroom and turned on the water. He didn't even wait for the water to warm. She could hear Frankie singing and whistling while he showered. This pleased her; she received the response she was looking for.

While Frankie was in the bathroom, she picked up his clothes and hung them up in the closet. She prepared the bed for them and lay down across the bed waiting for her husband. A few minutes later, Frankie came from the bathroom drying off. It was her turn to be surprised. His body was taut and his limbs just right. She could tell he was happy to be there with her.

"My, my, my," he said as he walked out the room seeing Areebah lying across the bed.

"Frankie, I love you. This is not at all how I planned my weekend."

They both laughed.

Thirty-Nine

"Well Salamah, Dad and Areebah are now married. You have to stop all of these evil actions," Jabari warned her as he walked into her room.

"I can't believe he really married her."

"Come on now, we can't be selfish. You have a boyfriend, I have a girlfriend; Yobachi and Chata are never home. Do you really want him to just sit around and be lonely?"

"I don't want him to be lonely, but why did he have to marry HER?"

"He's told you time and time again, he loves her. This is a lost love."

"Whatever."

"Put yourself in their shoes. What if you and your boyfriend broke up because his parents didn't want you to be together and years later you had the chance to be together, wouldn't you want to take that chance?"

"But his parents love me."

"But what if?"

"I guess. But I still think she is indirectly responsible for Mom's death."

"Even if she is, being rude and mean to her won't bring Mom back."

"I can't make any promises. Did he say when he was coming back?"

"No, he still has an open ticket."

"What about HER? Is SHE coming back with him?"

"He didn't mention it one way or the other."

"Okay, will you please close my door, I have something to do."

Jabari complied and closed the door. He was concerned about his sister. Her hate towards Areebah was unhealthy. Weeks after their mom died, she got into a fight at school. She slammed a girl's head into the floor so many times that the girl needed stitches. For whatever reason, she wasn't charged. She only got suspended from school for a few days. She didn't get into trouble because Frankie was in such a funk that he was not aware of the day-to-day situations with his children.

Jabari did not want Salamah to be violent towards Areebah if she did move with them. He needed to warn his dad. He knew that his father and Areebah were enjoying their wedding night, so he decided to wait until the morning to call and voice his concerns.

Forty

"As salaamu alaikum zawjati (my wife)," Frankie said as he awakened Areebah for Salatul Fajr.

"Wa laikum mus salaam, zawji (my husband)," Areebah said with a satisfied grin on her face.

"It's time to pray Baby, would you like to ghusl (shower after sexual intercourse) first or would you like me to go first?"

"I'll go first," Areebah said.

Last night was better than Frankie expected. They are compatible in every way. Just thinking about last night made him want to grab her out of the shower. Wait until after we pray. He consoled himself. However he thought or imagined his wedding night with her would be was one hundred times better. Alhamdulillah! Shukran Allah (thank you Allah)! He had to say because this was one of his best decisions in a long time.

Areebah walked out with two towels covering her, one for her head and one for her body. She looked even beautiful in the towels than she did in the lingerie. Frankie did all he could to control himself. Salat (prayer) is better than anything else at this time. He was thankful that salat only took a few minutes.

Frankie went into the bathroom and performed his ghusl. He planned on today being one of the cleanest days of his life because he planned on performing a lot of ghusls today.

I knew that Areebah was beautiful and although all of her clothes covered her, I had an idea that her body was beautiful. However, I didn't expect her to enjoy the wedding night as much as she did. I guess Muslim women are not as prudish as I thought.

Frankie walked out and Areebah avoided eye contact with him. He became concerned. He hoped he didn't do anything wrong or disappoint her.

"What's the matter Areebah?" Frankie said, scared to hear the response.

"I'm not looking at you because I'm ready to pray and I need to keep my mind focused on Allah subhana wa ta 'ala. I know if I look at you my desires will appear again."

Oh Yeah! "I understand. I just want to make sure you aren't disappointed that you married me."

"Disappointed, never, maa shaa Allah (it's

Allah's will)."

Frankie finished getting dressed and called the iqama (call to prayer). They performed Salatul Fajr (dawn prayer) and took time out to dhikr (remember) Allah and make du'a (supplication).

"Let's begin reading from the Qur'an together after Fajr," Areebah suggested.

"That's a great idea." Laurie and I never read the Bible or even discussed religion. This is a new experience for me.

Frankie and Areebah sat down and read the translation of Surah Al-Mulk (Chapter 67 – The Dominion) from the Qur'an. They then discussed what each person's perspective of the surah was. She then announced that she was hungry. He will soon come to find out that her most important meal was breakfast. She gets cranky and frustrated if she went too long in the morning without eating.

"We can order Room Service," he said wanting to get back in bed with his wife as soon as possible.

"That's a great idea," she went to the desk and picked up the Room Service menu.

"What would you like to eat?" She said.

"You decide," Frankie said as he marveled in her beauty.

The food arrived and they ate fried eggs over hard; multigrain toast with butter and strawberry jam; turkey bacon; and turkey sausage. For drinks she had orange juice and he had coffee. Just as she placed the tray out in the hallway, Frankie's phone rang.

Not again! Frankie thought back to the times when he and Laurie attempted the mini vacations. He let the phone ring and ring.

"Are you going to answer your phone?" She said wondering why he hesitated to answer it.

"My track record says when I'm out having a romantic time with my wife and the phone rings, the phone is bearer of bad news.

"But your children are home, across the country alone. It may be an emergency at home."

"Okay, I'll answer," he capitulated.

"Hello!"

"Hey Dad."

"Jabari, I thought I told you not to call me unless it was an emergency," Frankie said getting ticked off at his son.

"I know. I think this is an emergency. I really think Salamah is planning something to hurt Areebah when you two come home."

"What makes you think that?"

"She still blames Areebah for the cause of Mom's death. And remember when I told you about an earlier episode she had while you were out of it?"

"Yeah, I remember. Well, you don't have anything to worry about. Areebah isn't coming to live with us right away. Therefore I should be able to neutralize the situation before she comes to our house."

"Okay, but please Dad, I beg you. Let Salamah go get some psychological help. I truly think something is wrong with her."

"When I get back, I'll take her to the same place I went."

"Alright, I love you Dad. See you soon."

Frankie turned around and saw Areebah staring at him with a look of confusion. How can I tell her that my daughter doesn't like her and wants to do harm with her? This marriage was starting out so well; I don't want Salamah's antics causing fitnah (problems) in my marriage.

"Is everything okay?" Areebah said concerned.

"That was Jabari. He asked me when I am supposed to return. He's concerned about Salamah. She is finding it difficult accepting you as my wife."

"Sahlah is also having problems. I know what you're going through. What I think is that we need a united front. We let them know that we love them. However, this is our life and this is how we are deciding to live it."

"See, this is why I love you. Instead of freaking out that my daughter doesn't like you, you help find solutions."

"And by the way, when are you going back?"

"I haven't quite decided. I have a few more days off from work. But, I don't want to keep paying for a hotel room."

"But, why should you have to pay for a hotel room any longer. We are now married. I have a house, we can go there."

"I didn't even think about that. That's a great idea. Then, by Saturday I'll be leaving. This does bring me to another issue."

She turned around and he saw a look of concern on her face. Her look said that she knew what the next question would be.

"Are you moving with me?"

"I haven't thought about that. Remember prior to you coming here asking my dad for his blessing so you can marry me, you spoke with me sporadically and with little substance. As you know, I have my business here. I haven't thought about leaving the city yet. Maybe we can travel back and forth until we come up with an alternate plan."

"That sounds like an idea for a while. But Areebah, I didn't get married to be lonely. I want us to be together as husband and wife sooner than later."

"Frankie," she said with all sincerity, "Give me at least a month to figure things out."

"Okay, that's fair. Anyway, enough of that talk. You feel like taking another ghusl?"

"But of course."

Forty-One

Frankie headed back home. Leaving Areebah was bittersweet. He wanted more and more time with his wife. However, with her still in Philly, it gave Frankie the chance to get Salamah the help she needed as well as prepare his house for his new wife. Frankie was apprehensive about seeing his children. While he was happy to be married to Areebah, at times he felt the guilty twinge of being with someone other than Laurie. Sometimes Frankie wished Laurie was still there and they still had their good times.

Frankie fought back tears. His memories of Laurie were very strong. Although the last few months with Laurie were trying, the majority of their marriage was great. He thought back to the time when Laurie started unraveling and he still cannot figure what he could have done differently. Now that he's Muslim, he remembered reading something about the qadr of Allah, which is the divine will of Allah. He now realized that in order for him and Areebah to be together required both his wife and her husband to leave from the face of the earth.

Frankie boarded the plane with so many thoughts. Before he knew it he was sleep. As he stirred awake, he heard the captain say they were preparing to land. He didn't realize how tired he was. When the plane landed and the flight attendant stated it was okay to use the electronic devices, he called Jabari.

Ring. Ring. Ring.

"Hello. Dad?"

"Hey Son, are you here?"

"Just about, do you want me to meet you like I did last time?"

"No, this time meet me in baggage claim. I have more pieces of luggage so I decided to check all of my bags."

Frankie retrieved his luggage from baggage claim. Just as he stepped out of the door, Jabari drove up. Frankie's smile was so big that you could count all thirty-twos. He was happy to see his son. Jabari looked like he'd matured since Frankie's been gone.

"As salaamu alaikum Son."

"Hey Dad. You know I'm not Muslim."

"Not yet," Frankie said still smiling.

"I guess, Dad," Jabari said not amused.

"How's Salamah?" Frankie said disregarding

Jabari's listlessness.

"She seems like she's okay. However, I don't trust her façade."

"Well, at this time I do not know if Areebah is coming here to live. However, what I do know is that she told me she will give a more definitive answer in a month. Therefore, I have a month to get Salamah the help she needs. I can also prepare Chata and Yobachi for the arrival of my new wife."

"That sounds like a plan. How are you going to help Salamah?"

"Do you remember when your Aunt Felicia came when I was in my deep depression?"

"Yes, I am still thankful that she did that to get you out of your funk. I'd rather you be married to Areebah instead of depressed any time."

"Me too Son, me too; well, I'm going to take Salamah to that same facility. She needs professional help. That's the only way she can break out of her self-destructive ways."

"Dad, it sounds like a great plan. However, she may not go quietly and serenely as you did."

"Let me worry about her," Frankie said.

From the age of six months Salamah had a strong personality. Also, she was one who had horrible temper tantrums. It seemed like instead of growing out of the tantrums, she found other avenues in which to have a tantrum. Frankie's been handling her tantrums since she was an infant and he knew what to do when he got home.

"How are your brothers? Is there any news about them I need to know?"

"They're okay. However, I do think they have more freedom than they need."

"You're right. I've been neglectful of my children for far too long. It's time for me to go back being the dad I used to be."

"Thank you Dad. I've been waiting for this since Mom died."

Have I been that neglectful? I guess I have. I hope it's not too late. Maybe I was too quick on marrying Areebah. Why was I only thinking about myself? What have I done? Was it the right thing to marry her?

Ring. Ring. Ring.

"As salaamu alaikum."

"Wa laikum mus salaam, zawji. How are you?"

"I'm doing okay. I was just thinking about you."

"What were you thinking about? You sound distant. Is everything okay?"

"Do you think we rushed this marriage?"

"Why would you ask that Frankie?"

"I didn't take time to heal with my children and now I added someone new to our family."

"Are you telling me that you regret marrying me?"

"No, not at all; I'm just thinking about the time I neglected with my children."

"Frankie, listen to me. First of all, breathe.

Second of all, you still can take care of your family. I'm not here to make your life difficult. I'm here to enhance it. Also, remember that I love you."

"I love you too Areebah. Thank you for these words. I really was going down the great abyss."

"Remember that you can call me whenever. We are now husband and wife. I need to hear your voice and I'm sure you need to hear mine."

"You know I need more than to hear your voice. I need to take a ghusl a few times a week."

Frankie began to chuckle at his statement. He couldn't believe that less than a year ago he didn't even know what a ghusl was. Now he's using it to entice his wife. How he loved being married to Areebah.

"Me too," she said wishing he was with her right now.

"Have you given any more thought about moving with me?"

"You just left. I asked you to give me a month. But, yes, that's all I'm thinking about."

"I don't mean to pressure you. I just miss the feel of your body."

"Dad, Do I have to hear this?" Jabari said with disgust.

"Areebah, my son doesn't like to hear our mushy conversation. Let me call you when I'm alone in my room."

"I understand. I'll let you go. As salaamu alaikum. I love you."

"Wa laikum mus salaam, I love you too."

Frankie and Jabari arrived at the house an hour after leaving the airport. Traffic was heavy so it took longer than usual. Frankie was happy to return home. Although he enjoyed his time in Philly, he did miss his own bed. He also missed his children. Not wanting to move back to Philly, he decided that he's going to pray that Areebah decided to move with them. More importantly, he didn't want her up there with those brothers. Shaitan is always busy and Frankie didn't want any fitnah when it came to their marriage.

"Salamah! Chata! Yobachi! I'm home!" He bellowed as he opened the door.

"Daaad!" Chata and Yobachi screamed in unison. They ran down the stairs and hugged Frankie as if they hadn't seen him in years. As Frankie looked down on them, it does seem like they've grown a few inches since he's been gone. A sense of nostalgia entered his thoughts again. Laurie would have loved to see how the children were maturing.

Why did you have to crash into that tractor? I loved you so much. We could have worked out any issues we were having. I miss you Laurie.

"Salamah, where are you?" Frankie said since his daughter didn't come the first time he called her.

"What!"

This response caused Frankie to pause. I know this girl didn't just "What!" me. I better get her some help soon before I end up in the pen.

"What!! Is that the way you answer your father?"

"Well, you've been gone for so long. I'm starting to doubt if you're still my father."

"Jabari, Yobachi, and Chata, please leave us."

Hurrying out of the room, the boys looked back at their sister as if she grew a third eye and an extra head. None of them ever spoke to their father like she just did. They went upstairs and hid out of sight so they could eavesdrop on the conversation.

"First of all young lady, never, and I mean never speak with me in that tone of voice. Also, when I call you, the proper response is yes, not 'What!' Do you understand?"

"Yeah."

"Obviously not, Jabari told me that you've changed since your mom's death. But it is worse than I imagined."

"So now you recognize me? You weren't thinking about me when you went to marry Areebah!"

"Salamah," Frankie said with a calm he didn't feel, "go upstairs in your room and pack your suitcase with two weeks' worth of clothing. Include in your suitcase your cosmetics and any reading or writing material you need. I was going to hold off on getting you help for a couple of days, but evidently you need help right now."

"Really? You're sending me away."

"This is not up for discussion. Get up stairs now and do as instructed."

Salamah started upstairs mumbling under her breath and stomping up the steps.

"Come back down here right now," Frankie said with the same calm voice.

Salamah walked towards her dad rolling her eyes and sucking her teeth.

"Now, go upstairs and do as instructed."

Again, she stomped up the steps and mumbled under her breath.

"Come back again. Just to let you know. As long as you stomp up my steps, you will be going back and forth. So, try it again."

This time she went up the stairs without stomping. However, when she got to her room, she entered it and slammed the door.

"Pick your battles," Frankie reminded himself.

Allahu Akbar, Allahu Akbar! Allahu Akbar, Allahu Akbar!

The adhan for Salatul 'Asr called. Just in time. Frankie thought as he headed to his room so he could perform wudu. He needed the refreshing water to cool his anger. He needed the prayer to cool his soul. He could not believe how Salamah was behaving. Tough love is what she needed. But I feel guilty for falling into the depression and leaving my children to their own wiles, he berated himself.

Upon completion of offering his prayer, Frankie called Salamah. She was in a little better mood. However, she for sure needed to get BEAT, better education and training. While Salamah was in her room brooding, after he finished praying, Frankie contacted the facility so the transition for Salamah will be smooth.

"Salamah, are you ready?"

"Not yet."

"Okay, let me know when you're ready. You have thirty more minutes."

Frankie felt depression settling within him. He needed to talk to someone. Remembering what Areebah said, he decided to call her. He needed to hear her voice at this time.

"As salaamu alaikum Areebah. How are you?"

"Wa laikum mus salaam Frankie. I'm so glad you called me. I didn't want to be a bother. You sounded like you were having a jihad of the nafs."

"Jihad of the nafs? What's that?"

"That's an internal struggle. It seemed like something was bothering you when we last talked."

"It's amazing that you can already read my feelings. I was feeling a little guilty and nostalgic. I was missing Laurie and I continue to blame myself for her actions."

"I really understand. I never told you, but on our wedding night the reason I was in the bathroom so long is because guilty feelings rushed over me. Although I was able to spend the time with Murad as he was dying, Laurie's death was instantaneous and therefore is a lot more hurtful. Please remember that I am here for you for good and bad. Whenever you need an ear, please call me. How are the children?"

"That is a conversation we'll have to save for another time. I'm about to take Salamah to this facility and the answer to your question requires a lot of time. Well Areebah, I have to go, but I will call you when I return. I love you. As salaamu alaikum."

"I love you too. Wa laikum mus salaam."

"Really Dad, you love her?"

Salamah turned around and sulked out the room.

"Are we leaving yet?" She said.

Frankie shook his head and decided against saying anything else to Salamah at this time. They left the house for the facility. During the drive, Frankie tried to engage Salamah in a conversation to no avail. She was still sulking. Frankie prayed that this facility would able to assist her out of her anger and sadness. Then and only then will she resemble the Salamah prior to Laurie dying.

Forty-Two

"Wow, there are only a few more days left before I have to let Frankie know my decision regarding moving," Areebah told her mother concerned.

"I want to go; but, since moving back here I've been so involved in the community and my business is seeing a lot of success. What do you suggest?"

"Well, Sweetheart, this is a decision you must make. This is your life. The best suggestion I can give you is to make 'Istikhara prayer and wait for an answer from Allah subhana wa ta 'ala."

"I understand that. I know that is the best way. However, whenever I make 'Istikhara, the answer arrives quickly. I'm not sure if I'm ready for the answer."

"Ask yourself these questions Areebah. 'Do I want to live with my husband continuously or do

I want the women at the masjid where he lives to think that there is a new man without a wife there? If I move, will it stop me from being involved in the community? What sacrifices am I willing to make if I make this move?"

"Ummi, I always appreciate your insight. I will perform 'Istikhara as well as reflect on what I want. I have to go now. I'll talk to you later, in shaa Allah."

Areebah disconnected the phone from her mother and sat for a few more minutes contemplating her next steps. She so loved Frankie but she was not sure if she was ready to uproot herself again. She was not sure if she wanted to stay in Philly. She acquiesced and performed Salatul 'Istikhara.

Areebah decided to call Frankie. Hearing his voice always made her calm down.

Ring. Ring. Ring.

"As salaamu alaikum Areebah. How are you today?"

"Wa laikum mus salaam. I'm a little apprehensive."

"What are you apprehensive about?"

"The month is almost up and I still haven't given you an answer regarding me moving down there."

"Let me see if I can make it easy for you."

"How can you make it easy for me?"

"There was an opening at the Philadelphia branch of my company. They needed some people to move. They provide moving expenses as well as an increase in salary. Looks like you don't have to decide to move here."

Alhamdulillah! Areebah couldn't believe what she was hearing. La hawla quwatta wa illah billah (There is no power or might greater than Allah).

"How do the children feel about this move?"

"Honestly, I could care less how they feel. However, they all seem happy. Maybe it is what is needed for a fresh start. We'll be moving in a couple of weeks. I need you to scope out a nice house where the schools are pretty decent. I am anxious to get our new lives started."

"As am I. As am I. Frankie, I love you so much for making this decision. I know it had to be difficult. I am sure that it was a struggle. I just want to let you know that I appreciate everything that you do."

"Areebah, I love you and as I reflect back on our past, I realize that I always loved you. This was one of the easiest decisions I've had to make in a long time. How I long to be with you."

"Frankie, I love you more than ever. I'm counting the days until you arrive. Let me go now so I can start searching for houses for us. Oh, by the way, what's the price range I'm looking at?"

"Anywhere between $200,000 and $250,000."

"Okay," Areebah said. However, in her mind she was already deciding where they may live. For one thing, it will not be in Philadelphia.

"Well, I have to go. I love you and will talk to

you later tonight Areebah. As salaamu alaikum."

"Wa laikum mus salaam. I love you also. Talk to you soon, in shaa Allah."

Areebah disconnected the call and sat on the musalah, prayer rug, and began praising and thanking Allah. Her mother told her to perform Salatul 'Istikhara. She is thankful that she did.

Ring. Ring. Ring.

"As salaamu alaikum Areebah, twice in a day? For what do I owe this call?" Kashifah said intrigued.

"Ummi, you will never believe this. I performed Salatul 'Istikhara as you suggested. After praying I sat silently and reflected on my life. I then decided to call Frankie. Guess what happened?"

"What? Did he beg for you to move there now instead of waiting for the entire month?"

"Not at all, he told me that his job is opening a branch in Philadelphia and that they asked if anyone was interested in relocating in Philadelphia."

"SubhanAllah. See the power of prayer?"

"Na'am. When I got off the phone with him, I sat in reflection and prayer."

"Maa shaa Allah. Well, you did say that your prayers are generally answered, this shows how clean and clear your heart is."

"Is he bringing the entire clan?"

"Yes, and they will be here within two weeks."

"SubhanAllah! Two weeks, and he and his

family will meet me here so we can start our next chapter in life."

"I'm really happy for you Areebah. But, on top of that, I'm happy for your father and me. We don't have to lose our baby again," Kashifah said with a tremble in her voice.

"Ummi? Are you crying?"

"I'm just a little emotional. I have to go now. Please call me later, in shaa Allah," she said rushing off the phone.

"Okay, in shaa Allah. As salaamu alaikum."

"Wa laikum mus salaam my beautiful daughter."

As Kashifah was disconnecting the phone, Areebah believed that she heard her mother crying. *I'm glad it worked out like this. Ummi puts up a good face. However, I know she wants me here; especially since her age is progressing.*

Forty-Three

"Honey, I'm home!" Frankie yelled as he greeted the house.

"As salaamu alaikum Baby. Welcome home?" Areebah rushed into Frankie's arms as he and the children arrived with the moving truck.

"How was the trip?"

"It was eventful. It took longer than anticipated. However, we got to see so much of our beautiful country."

"How about the children, did they enjoy themselves? Are they excited about moving here?"

"Well…for the most part, yes."

"Is Salamah still having problems?"

"Just a little, but I think we can work through it."

Just then, the children walked into the house. After touring the house, they all appeared pleased.

"I'm so happy you all like the house. I think you will like the schools that you'll start this week. I look forward to us growing together as a family."

Silence swept through the house. Each person looked at the other. No one knew what the next step was. Areebah, sensing the apprehension, decided to be the first one to speak.

"In the kitchen I have a fantastic dinner prepared. There is barbecue chicken, cheese broccoli, rice, salad, cake, and ice cream. There are also a variety of drinks. I am sure after the long trip that you are ready for some home cooked food."

Salamah was the first to head to the kitchen. Areebah, Frankie, and Jabari looked at each other because she had a smile on her face. Maybe this was the beginning of something new and good. Everyone else headed to the kitchen and sat down and ate. The next chapter in everyone's life was ready to begin.

ABOUT THE AUTHOR

Karimah Grayson is a Muslim American author. Originally from Philadelphia, PA, Karimah resides in Fort Lauderdale, FL. The love of water and the beautiful blue skies keeps her loving the Sunshine State. By profession she is an educator and enjoys watching her students mature into adulthood. Karimah recently began writing in the little known genre of Muslim fiction and looks forward to sharing the Muslim American experience with the world.

You can follow Karimah on the following social media sites:

Facebook - https://www.facebook.com/KGAuthor
Facebook -
https://www.facebook.com/AreebahsDilemmaNovel
Twitter - https://twitter.com/AuthorKarimahG
Pinterest -
https://www.pinterest.com/AuthorKarimah
LinkedIn -
https://www.linkedin.com/in/karimahgrayson
Instagram - https://instagram.com/authorkarimahg
Visit her blog and website at:
https://authorkarimahg.wordpress.com
http://authorkarimahg.wix.com/muslimfiction

Visit her author pages at:
https://www.goodreads.com/author/show/1412618
2.Karimah_Grayson
http://www.amazon.com/author/karimahgrayson

THE
SHOULDERS ON
WHICH I STAND

Karimah
Grayson

ONE

Rushing from the third staff meeting of the week, Daria darted through the groups of students. As she approached the classroom door, her students gathered around her asking many questions. She turned around and pointed for the students to line up against the wall. They knew her procedure they needed to enter her classroom in an orderly fashion.

After the students entered the classroom, she turned on the television tuned into the morning announcements and recited the Pledge of Allegiance. Although she didn't agree with the pledge, she encouraged the students to stand and be respectful. As soon as the morning announcements ended, Daria turned towards the students and wondered why so many hands were up.

"Yes Travante?"

"Miss, when are we going to learn African-American History again? Do we have to wait for Black History month? I want to learn about Martin Luther King, Rosa Parks, and Harriett Tubman?" Travante said for the third time this week.

It never surprised Daria each time the students asked about learning African-American History. They always wanted to learn about the holy trinity of Africa-American History.

"First of all, let's get this straight," Daria said folding her arms across her chest. "African-Americans are part of the woven fiber of this country. Therefore, when I teach you, it will not just include Martin Luther King, Jr., Rosa Parks, and Harriett Tubman."

"But Miss, they're the reason we are free and can ride the bus," Charlene said looking Daria straight in the eyes.

"Let's think about that statement," Daria said counting to ten in her head. Year after year she has different students who ask the same question. She's not frustrated with the students; the frustrating part is that these students are now in the eleventh grade and the only African-Americans they can name are the holy trinity.

"But Miss," Travante began, "I remember being taught that if it wasn't for Martin Luther King, Jr. none of us would be free."

"Before we talk about Dr. Martin Luther King, Jr., who can tell me about El Hajj Malik El Shabazz?" Daria said

"Who?" The class said in unison looking from one to the other.

"You may have heard of him as Malcolm X," Daria said with a chuckle.

"Oh, him!" June said as she raised her hand.

"He was a slave, right?"

"A slave, why do you say he was a slave June?" Daria said not understanding the response.

"Because his last name is X and that was to get rid of his slave name," June said raising her right eyebrow.

Daria laughed aloud when she heard this. She was surprised that June knew about slave names. However, it bothered her that out of all of her students only one heard of him and her information is incorrect.

"June, excellent use of context clues; now I

understand why you thought he was a slave. You are correct; the 'X' was used to replace the slave name. But that doesn't mean he was a slave. Let me see if I can help you understand. Your last name is Jones, right June?"

"Yes."

"Okay, the Jones last name came from the slave master. Generally you do not see people from the different African countries with the last name of Jones."

"But Miss," June said, "my parents aren't slaves."

"Correct, they aren't because slavery ended for most slaves in 1865. However, the Jones surname came from the slave masters of your ancestors."

"Surname? Miss, why do you use such hard words? What is a surname?"

"Surname is another word for last name. Remember, I told you I'm here to educate you. This education includes increasing your vocabulary. Now back to Malcolm X. Before he was Malcolm X, he was Malcolm Little. That being said, does anyone else know anything about him?"

"Wait Miss, what about the name El Hajj Malik El Sh…or whatever you said," Jose said.

"I'm glad you picked up on that Jose. Near the end of his life, he accepted Islam and changed his name to Malik El-Shabazz. After performing the hajj, which is the pilgrimage to Mecca that all Muslims must make at least once in their lifetime, the moniker El Hajj was added to his name."

"Here she goes again with those big words," Travante said louder than necessary.

"What is a moniker Miss?" June said enthralled with the conversation.

"I'm glad you asked," Daria said happy to see her students picking up on the unfamiliar words. "A moniker is a title one selects for oneself."

"I remember hearing that he used to be a Muslim and he stopped," said Lincoln.

"Well, you're almost right. He was in the Nation of Islam; this is a Black Nationalist movement whose teachings went against many of the tenets of Al-Islam. As he studied and learned more about Al-Islam, he realized that what he was taught was not Al-Islam so he left the Nation of Islam and testified his faith as a follower of Al-Islam. Not long afterward, he made the pilgrimage to Hajj in Saudi Arabia."

"But Miss, what does he have to do with African American history?" Amelia piped in.

"Well, as Martin Luther King, Jr. and Rosa Parks encouraged non-violence, Malcolm X believed in self-defense 'By any means necessary'."

"I don't understand Miss, what does 'By any means necessary mean?" Zariah said holding her head to the side

"What it means Zariah is that instead of turning the other cheek, Malcolm X believed in defending himself. This is why he was as important as the other three you mentioned. But, I want you all to know that there are many people and organizations that were as relevant in American History."

"This is very interesting Miss, I didn't know anything you just told me. Why aren't we taught this in other classes?" LaTasha said.

That's a continuous question Daria had. Why indeed are students taught only about the holy trinity of African American History? Why isn't African American History included in the lessons in regular American History since there have been Africans here before the Mayflower and beyond?

"LaTasha, what a fantastic question, but as a character in the movie said, 'It doesn't matter, it's in the past.' We cannot focus on what you didn't learn. What we will do this school year is focus on what you will learn."

The students stood up and began applauding and cheering. In order not to have the administration come to her classroom, Daria quieted the students and made them sit back down.

"This school year we're going to learn American History and incorporate all of the people involved in the development of this great country of ours. Often we make the US as if it is a dichotomous society…"

Daria looked around and saw some students with the look of befuddlement while others raised their hands as soon as she said the word waiting for her to call on them.

"Yes Jean?"

"What is a dicho… Uh, dichotot…I don't know how to say it. But the word you just said."

"I'm so proud of you raising your hand and asking that question Jean. The word is dichotomous which means two specific groups of people. Now class, please repeat the word after me. Di cho to mous."

"Di cho to mous," they said in unison. Daria heard some students mispronounce the word.

"Okay, one more time. I didn't hear everyone and some of you are saying it incorrectly. Repeat after me, di cho to mous."

"Di cho to mous," they repeated again.

"Much better," Daria said. "What I mean is that the United States was never just black and white. There have been multiple ethnicities and races of people involved in the growth and development of this country."

"For example, you will learn about how the Chinese were important in the building of the railroads. This country has a rich history and we all are integral parts of the history."

"Miss, I like your class. Do we have any homework?" Antoine said as he looked at the clock.

"As always Antoine, the homework is written on the board. Make sure you write it down in your agenda. Well, class, the bell is about to ring. Make sure to gather all of your belongings and I will release you when the bell rings."

Riiinnnggg!

"Okay class, I will see you tomorrow. Have a wonderful evening."

Made in the USA
Charleston, SC
28 June 2016